SHE DID NOT KNOW SHE WAS ABOUT TO
BECOME A PAWN IN THE ROLLICKING—
AND DANGEROUS—GAME OF LOVE...

Wager for Love

Rachelle Edwards

FAWCETT COVENTRY • NEW YORK

WAGER FOR LOVE

Published by Fawcett Coventry Books, a unit of CBS Publications, the Consumer Publishing Division of CBS Inc., by arrangement with Robert Hale Limited

ISBN: 0-449-50021-7

THIS BOOK CONTAINS THE COMPLETE TEXT OF THE ORIGINAL HARDCOVER EDITION.

Printed in the United States of America

First Fawcett Coventry printing: January 1980

10 9 8 7 6 5 4 3 2 1

One

Sir Hugo Lytton tossed and turned rest-
lessly in his four-poster bed, but the uncomfortable dream would not fade. However
hard he struggled against them a horde of
determined women still pursued him in his
slumber.

There was, of course, a good reason for
his restlessness; the Social Season was
growing old and for once he was heartily
weary of it, or rather, weary of evading the
wiles of husband-seeking debutantes and
their equally determined mothers.

Suddenly he awoke with a start and after
gazing around the shadowy room in bewil-
derment for a moment or two, with a sigh of
relief he sank back into the pillows, which
were embroidered with the coat of arms of
the Lytton family as was the bed's silk
tester and counterpane.

It was past dawn and noises were
emanating from both within the house and
the street outside. The servants would have

been astir for a long time but it was very early for a gentleman such as Sir Hugo to be awake, especially as he had not returned home until the early hours of the morning, and he wondered what had awoken him so precipitously. Certainly sleep was gone and he was now wide awake, happy to reflect on an evening gaming successfully with a number of his cronies at Brooks's and a subsequent visit to his current mistress.

As if in answer to his unspoken thoughts a few stones rattled against the window-pane. Frowning, Sir Hugo got out of bed and struggled into his brocade dressing gown. As he did so another shower of stones hit his window. He hurried across the room to the window which overlooked Mount Street in Mayfair, ready to hurl a stream of abuse at whoever had the impudence to disturb his slumber. One hand thrust back the heavy damask curtain to allow early morning light to flood into the room. He blinked at the intensity of it and then pushed up the sash window. As he peered down into the courtyard below his countenance cleared, recognising the carriage of Viscount Devaney who had been a close friend of his since schooldays.

Friend or not, he was nevertheless heartily displeased to see the young man. "What the devil do you think you are about at this time of the morning?" he demanded.

Lord Devaney stood back and looked at him. "I must talk to you, Hugo. It is of the utmost import."

"Nothing is important enough to disturb my rest so come back at a respectable hour."

Sir Hugo withdrew his head but as he did so Lord Devaney shouted, "I'm in a fix, Hugo, and it won't wait."

Sir Hugo sighed and looked out of the window once more. "And not for the first time. Well, come along up and order some chocolate before you do."

Lord Devaney gave him a woeful smile. "I could take something a mite stronger."

"*Chocolate,*" Sir Hugo reiterated before slamming down the window.

A few minutes later Lord Devaney was shown into Sir Hugo's room. He had been divested of his greatcoat and was still wearing evening dress. Sir Hugo eyed him critically, noting that his shoes were scuffed and muddy and his breeches far from immaculate, which was a rare lapse for someone as fastidious as Lord Devaney.

"Well, Dev, what fix are you in this time? Want to beg the blunt? Or escape an irate husband?"

"Oh, I wish you would not jest." The young man wrung his hands together. "May I sit down? It's been the devil of a night."

Sir Hugo allowed himself a small smile. "So it appears. I cannot recall when I last saw you looking so...dishabille. By all means do sit down and tell me all about it. I am sure that is exactly what you intend to do," he added drily.

As the young man seated himself in a wing chair a manservant arrived with cups of steaming chocolate which Lord Devaney eyed with disdain and Sir Hugo sipped with relish. The manservant cast a disapproving eye over Lord Devaney before attending his master once more.

"Will there be anything more you require, Sir Hugo?"

"Not at the moment, Cunningham, but you might put out my new coat and the buff waistcoat. I doubt if I shall return to bed. I'll ring when I need you again."

As the manservant withdrew Sir Hugo seated himself in a chair facing his friend. "Apparently you haven't been home yet."

"There has been no opportunity. I dined at Silverwood House yesterday..."

"Ah yes, I was invited but was obliged to cry off owing to a previous engagement."

For the first time since his arrival Lord Devaney grinned. "I can hazard a guess with whom. Mrs Chatsley's a fine actress, Hugo."

"And a fine woman too. However..."

Lord Devaney's smile faded. "Remington was at Silverwood House—m'sister has a fancy for him. Well...Remington invited a few of us back to his house for a little play afterwards..."

"Little! Dev, Remington plays deep at every hand. Do you not know him?"

Lord Devaney looked abashed. "We were all a trifle foxed by that time."

Sir Hugo gave a sigh of resignation before smiling at his friend. "So that is the way of it. How much did you lose?"

"I didn't. I won a few guineas."

"A few?"

A fleeting smile crossed the young man's face. "A few thousand..."

Sir Hugo drew in a sharp breath. "Remington was not happy about that, I'll wager."

"He was foxed out of his mind by that

time. Accused me of marking the cards. Hugo, I ask you, what would you have done?"

The other man gazed steadily at his friend, his blue eyes darkening almost to black. "I would have refused his invitation in the first instance." Lord Devaney averted his eyes and Sir Hugo went on resignedly, "So you called him out."

"Had no choice, Hugo. Matter of honour, y'know."

"The longer I know you, Dev, the more convinced I become that your attic's to let. This is the most insane thing you've done since you rode a horse into Lord Maldinch's drawing room!"

"That was only a lark, Hugo."

"I assume you wish me to act as second on your behalf when this folly takes place."

Lord Devaney looked up sharply. "No such thing! The duel took place this morning. Cranbourne and Fitch were my seconds."

Sir Hugo stared at him in amazement before saying, "You didn't surely kill him."

"Put a ball in his arm. You should have seen his face! Beaten twice in one night! I believe that hurt more than the injury."

"It would and much as I like the idea of

Remington paid back in his own coin, I must remind you, Dev, that there could be repercussions. Remington is not what I would deem an honourable man. You've both broken the law which is no laughing matter."

"Lord, yes, that is why I came straight to you. I knew *you'd* give me good advice. I left the others babbling away to each other. Remington's fond Mama won't let this matter lie. She's bound to want revenge for her son's humiliation."

"Assuming Remington will tell her how he came by his injury. If I were in his place I own I would remain silent on the matter."

"*You* are a different stamp of a man. He'll go whining to her, just as he always does whenever things go wrong for him. He lost so much last night he'll be obliged to beg the blunt from her. It's no use; I shall just have to go to the continent."

The thought obviously gave him no joy. "No doubt I shall die there of some unspeakable disease!"

Sir Hugo was forced to smile. "You managed to survive your grand tour—and even enjoy it." The young man refused to be cheered and his friend went on, "I don't really believe such drastic action is needed,

Dev. A short sojourn in the country and the trouble will have been forgotten."

Lord Devaney looked unconvinced. "Do you really think so?"

"Lady Remington may be many things, but she really is no fool and if she insists upon prolonging this matter she will discover it does not reflect too well on her beloved son being incapably drunk, playing too deep and losing a duel all in the course of one evening. She will not want *that* known abroad."

"But rusticating at the height of the Season will be as bad as going to the continent. Dash it all, it's too much to ask of a fellow."

Sir Hugo threw back his head and laughed heartily. "Why is it *your* sins never come home to roost?"

"Oh, I am certain that they will one day." More soberly he added, "In my opinion, it really is imperative that you leave Town for a while, Dev. If the law comes to hear of it you'll be sampling the delights of Newgate. Better boredom than incarceration." He paused before asking, "Would you find the thought of rusticating more congenial if I were to come with you?"

"Oh, I would not ask that of you."

"You didn't. I am offering to accompany you."

"I can't think why you should."

"Perchance we shall both benefit from a spell in the country."

Lord Devaney shook his head. "I'm persuaded I shall be forced to go but it's too much to expect of you at the height of the Season, Hugo."

Sir Hugo waved his hand impatiently in the air. "What does the Season mean? A horde of young ladies fresh out of the schoolroom attempting to ensnare a husband. I am tired of it. It has become irksome avoiding their simpering attentions and even more obnoxious are the machinations of their mothers. It seems that as I grow older they become more persistent and devious. Do you know what happened on the evening before last at Lady Torrington's rout?"

"I cannot imagine," Lord Devaney answered with great relish.

"Mrs Coatesworth insisted upon following me from room to room ..."

"Josiah Coatesworth is a man of considerable means even if he is in Trade."

"It is not Mr. Coatesworth I object to. His wife eventually confided she had a problem and pressed me to meet her in the arbour to discuss a matter of the utmost import, and what do you think happened?"

Lord Devaney grinned despite his preoccupation with his own problems. "*Miss* Coatesworth was waiting instead."

"Is there no end to their devious ways?"

"Not until you're leg-shackled, I fear. You are very eligible, Hugo, and I know of at least six hopeful beauties who declare themselves in love with you."

Sir Hugo made a noise of derision and Lord Devaney added, "You could do worse than choose one of them as your bride."

"I could scarce do worse."

"I intend to marry one day. I owe it to my family to do so and so do you. You have the advantage over me in that you are able to choose where you will. I must needs marry an heiress but you can pick where you will."

Sir Hugo waved an indolent hand in the air. "No doubt I shall marry one day and for the reason you mentioned, but it will not be until I am too old and feeble to find my pleasures elsewhere.

"However, Dev, we are not here to discuss my plans for the future. It is yours we must settle and quickly. It would be best if you were out of Town before the news is spread of the duel. It suits me to escape the pursuit of the young debutantes and you to evade any ensuing scandal. Where shall it be? Your place or mine?"

The young man became thoughtful and his friend continued to look at him, a sardonic smile playing at the corners of his lips. "Elspeth's place," Lord Devaney said at last. "She's been asking me to attend to some matters on her behalf so this would be an ideal opportunity of doing so." He sighed deeply. "Dev'lish dull, my sister's place. I wish she would marry again. Elspeth's too fetching to remain a widow."

He eyed Sir Hugo somewhat speculatively but when he received no answer he went on, "No need for you to come, Hugo. It would be a pity to separate you from Mrs Chatsley just now."

"Oh, I doubt if she will be lonely in my absence," Sir Hugo answered airily.

His friend was too abashed to answer but in an embarrassed tone said, "I would hate for my foolishness to reflect upon you."

Sir Hugo was already getting to his feet and reaching for the bell pull. He was all of six feet tall and as one lady admirer once remarked, as dark as Satan. He, like most fashionable men of the *haute monde*, preferred the freedom of not wearing a wig except on the most formal occasions, and instead wore his hair tied back with a ribbon.

"I have sent for Cunningham," he told his friend, "and we can leave for the Silverwood estate as soon as I am dressed." He smiled suddenly. "This opportunity is unforeseen and unfortunate but nevertheless I shall look forward to it, for it is many years since I was there."

Wryly Lord Devaney replied, "You must have forgotten how dull it is."

"After last night and this morning should you not welcome it?" When he recieved no reply, he added, "You will feel better for knowing you have done your sister a service, and more importantly we shall be out of Town before the tongues begin to wag!"

Two

"Lady Silverwood has quite an imposing parcel of land here," Sir Hugo observed one day as they rode back from a meeting with that lady's land steward.

"She did well from her marriage to old Silverwood, but of course, as you know, she has rarely visited his seat since he died. Elspeth is not a countrywoman at heart. She much prefers the amusements that Town has to offer and after the Season is over she will venture only as far as Tunbridge to take the waters."

"I cannot imagine why," his friend replied, inhaling deeply. "There is nothing more enjoyable and bracing than the pleasures of one's own country estate."

Lord Devaney eyed him thoughtfully. "I believe you are a countryman at heart, which is something I had never considered before. You would do well to settle down to country living—once you have a wife, naturally. A house such as Lytton Abbey is ideal for family life."

"The sentiment your remarks conjure up almost brings tears to my eyes," his friend remarked ironically.

"You are a hard-hearted man, Hugo."

"Just a freedom-loving one."

"I do wish Elspeth would wed again."

"Lady Silverwood has suitors enough."

Lord Devaney glanced at his friend who was astride a coal black mare and although he wore riding clothes contrived, somehow, to look as elegant as he did in the salons of the *ton*.

"Come now, Hugo, you must know there is only the one man she would marry."

"You are fanciful," Sir Hugo replied, laughing, but there was an uncharacteristic note of discomfort in his manner.

"Not I! I know my own sister. Grant me that, Hugo."

"We have always been the greatest of friends," Sir Hugo replied in a muted tone.

It was his friend's turn to laugh. "Friendship! You once paid her court, before she wed Silverwood."

"She was the Toast of the Town that Season, Dev, and it was expected of every one of us to vie for her favours, but Silverwood offered first and was accepted."

"You are older now, though. Your giddy youth is behind you."

"Long ago," Sir Hugo answered drily.

"I know she is my own sister, but I'm not mistaken, am I? You can find no fault in her demeanour."

"Lady Silverwood is a great beauty and I am very fond of her." He turned slightly in the saddle to look at Lord Devaney. "Why are you suddenly so anxious to find me a wife?"

Lord Devaney grinned wickedly. "Perchance, I don't like to see a man so well-pleased with himself."

Sir Hugo laughed and urged his mare into a trot, saying over his shoulder, "Lady Silverwood may be fetching enough to put the fever in any man's blood, but it would be a brave one indeed who would take on your niece as a step-daughter."

His friend laughed too. 'By gad, you're right, Hugo! I'd never thought of that."

They rode on at a trot for a while until the old grey pile of Silverwood House came into view. "Lady Silverwood cannot know what she is missing," Sir Hugo remarked as he surveyed the vista of trees and fields in which the house nestled. "She ought to bring her cronies here for a visit and rediscover the delights of rusticating."

"She might consider the notion if you were to suggest it and offer to accompany her." He turned his head, frowning slightly. "What is that I hear?"

"Hounds baying, I believe. Lady Silverwood's pack?"

Lord Devaney shook his head. "Elspeth doesn't keep a pack any more. It must be Squire Chawton's pack. He has the only one hereabouts."

Sir Hugo rose in the saddle to look around him. "I can see them in the distance, over there."

As he pointed his friend continued to frown. "The hunt never comes this close to Silverwood. Squire Chawton usually hunts at the other side of his estate."

"They appear to be coming closer."

"That is truly odd."

"There is something odder, Dev. Look, you can see them now. There are no more than a half dozen of them and they don't appear dressed for the hunt."

"Squire Chawton is an odd fellow. Silverwood never did make much to-do with him. Far from being a gentleman, Chawton's an unsavoury character from all I have learned. However, they will not cross the river. Any sign of the quarry? Those hounds seem hard on the scent."

"Indeed, they are, but I can see no sign of a fox or a hare." He paused. "I saw something moving in the thicket but I am sure it was too big to be a fox."

"Unlikely too as that thicket is well inside Silverwood land." His lips formed into a thin line. "To the devil with Chawton. This is Elspeth's land and that's a poacher in there. It must be a poacher!"

He was all set to go in pursuit but his friend held back the bridle. "It might only have been a shadow, Dev. I cannot be sure."

"The devil take it! I saw something moving myself. Come on, Hugo. We'll bag the fellow ourselves and see him hang!"

Lord Devaney surged forward with Sir Hugo in pursuit close behind. When they reached the thicket Lord Devaney jumped from his horse and would have plunged in without pause, only Sir Hugo held him back.

"Have a care, Dev. If there is a poacher in there he may be armed and with nothing to lose. He will hang whether he kills you or not."

"We cannot wait to summon the game-keepers, for we shall lose him and that I am not prepared to risk." He glanced over his shoulder with an uneasy look. "Those hounds are close. What the devil is that old reprobate about?"

"It really is no concern of ours. As you say

they will not cross the river so let us attend to this little matter."

He tethered their horses to a tree and they went into the thicket on foot, walking gingerly lest they alert the poacher to their presence. Birds flying from branch to branch caused them to draw back from time to time, but at last Sir Hugo espied a figure stealthily moving between the trees and he indicated silently to his companion the direction they were to take. Behind them the baying of the hounds was growing louder but for the moment the two gentlemen were oblivious to it.

Their own quarry could just about be seen cowering behind the wide trunk of an oak tree. As poachers were a real scourge Lord Devaney smiled at the prospect of capturing one, something usually achieved by the gamekeeper although not nearly often enough. Both men moved forward with equal stealth, anxious not to startle their quarry.

"Don't move from there," Lord Devaney ordered when they were but a few yards away.

A head turned to look at them in response to the order, a white face wide-eyed with fear, and at the sight of it both men were completely taken aback.

"'Tis a wench!" Lord Devaney cried.

Sir Hugo said nothing. He could only stare in astonishment at the shivering creature clinging to the tree trunk. Her gown was sodden and clinging to her boyish figure. It was torn in several places and there was blood about her face and shoulders where hedge and bramble had torn at her flesh. Likewise her bare feet were bloodstained and what might in other circumstances be a glorious mane of golden hair was matted with dirt and leaves.

At the sight of them she began to whimper, edging away until Sir Hugo roused himself once more and stepped forward a pace. "Don't be afraid. We will not hurt you. Who are you? What are you doing here?"

"Don't...let...them get...me," she pleaded, glancing back the way she had come.

Lord Devaney frowned. "Surely the hounds cannot be after *you*."

She nodded, her eyes still full of fear. Her entire body was trembling with terror.

The young man stiffened with indignation. "That is diabolical. What did you do to warrant it?"

The girl's eyes darted fearfully this way and that. "No...thing."

"Well, you have nothing to fear from them now. This is Silverwood land and they will not cross on to it, be assured."

But, it seemed, the girl was not assured in the least for the baying of the hounds was louder and she began to back away from them. Lord Devaney took a step forward too.

"Why are they hounding you?"

She stared at them as if assessing their trustworthiness and Sir Hugo supposed their appearance in such fine apparel decided her that they were foes too. Turning on her heel she attempted to flee once more but stumbled on a root only a few yards away before crumbling into a heap on the ground.

Sir Hugo and Lord Devaney immediately hurried to her as she lay insensible on the ground. "Poor child," Lord Devaney murmured. "What an abominable experience. We must help her."

He looked to his friend who was staring down at the girl, for confirmation, but Sir Hugo said, "Save your sympathy, Dev. We don't know as yet why Squire Chawton is so anxious to find her. In other words she may be guilty of some crime."

"Does that matter? She is no more than a

child...to be hunted like an animal. From what I have heard of Chawton he is a slimy old reprobate." His face grew red with anger. "Dash it all, Hugo, you can't mean us to leave her here. *I* have no intention of doing so!"

Sir Hugo smiled, albeit faintly. "Save your spleen, Dev. Fetch the horses and she can ride before me."

Lord Devaney looked more satisfied but as he went to fetch the horses he hesitated. "Do you think she is badly hurt?"

Sir Hugo glanced at her again before shaking his head. "I'll wager, it is only a swoon."

When, a minute or two later, Lord Devaney returned with the horses Sir Hugo had wrapped the unfortunate girl in his own coat and was ready to lift her onto his mare.

As they left the thicket the hounds were at the banks of the river trying to find the scent of their quarry.

"My God, I wish I could mete out the same treatment to him!" Lord Devaney fumed.

"As I said earlier," his friend answered blandly, "we have no notion what she has done."

"I'll warrant nothing serious."

Sir Hugo spurred the horse on faster whilst the hounds bayed hopelessly on the far bank. "No doubt we shall find out in due course," he said, almost to himself.

Charles Devaney smiled delightedly as he closed the door of the library behind him. Walking across the floor, he rubbed his hands together briskly.

"Mrs Noakes says the girl has recovered from her swoon, has only superficial scratches and should recover fully after a rest."

"That is a mercy," Sir Hugo replied.

His booted feet were resting on the desk and he held a glass of madeira in his hand. A fire crackled in the hearth and Lord Devaney crossed the room to warm his hands at it.

"It was fortunate we came upon her when we did, Hugo, for who is to know what would have been her fate if we had not."

"Upon that we cannot speculate but what to do with her now, Dev?" Sir Hugo asked, arching his eyebrow.

His friend shrugged as he straightened up from the fire. "We shall have to wait until she recovers and hear her story."

Sir Hugo held up his glass to the light of a candelabrum where several candles flickered. "And if Squire Chawton will not be so obliging as to wait also?"

"He cannot possibly know she is here."

"He is like to make enquiries. She might well be a felon or escaped from an asylum."

"You can be sure I will not turn her over to *him* whatever her crime."

"I suspect, my friend, you have already decided her innocence, but you should be wary of doing so simply because the chit is fair of face."

Lord Devaney looked outraged. "Hugo, would I be so foolish?" His friend's answer was merely a chuckle and, affronted, Lord Devaney asked, "Is your coat utterly ruined?"

"I fear that it is, but it is of no real matter. I was tired of it anyway. I shall see my tailor when I return to Town."

He leaned forward to pour more madeira into his glass and then filled one for his companion who when he came to take it smiled warmly.

"You are a good friend to me, Hugo, although there are times when I am aware that your patience is sorely tried. I know I am impulsive whereas you pause to consider everything fully."

"No doubt you also find me a trifle

irksome at times, Dev," Sir Hugo answered magnanimously.

"Indeed I do not! My admiration for you is endless. I shall never cease to wish I could be as urbane as you. Your tongue has such a sharp edge to it I often wish I too could be as biting. Not only that, you have such..."

"Oh, spare my blushes," Sir Hugo answered indolently. "What *are* you going to do about your...guest upstairs? What shall you do if you discover she has...say, set about her family with an axe?"

"Oh, really, Hugo, do be serious!"

One of Sir Hugo's dark eyebrows rose a fraction. "I am being perfectly serious I assure you."

Lord Devaney smiled foolishly. "That young girl could not have harmed anyone. An axe indeed!"

Sir Hugo shook his head slowly from side to side. "Do you really believe one has to be *ugly* to commit a serious crime? I had credited you with more sense." He wagged one finger at his disbelieving friend. "A year or two ago I attended an execution at Tyburn. One of those who was hanged that day just happened to be a girl of very tender years—Rose Bluett. She had murdered her lover with an axe and then set about the landlord in a like manner. Let me assure you, Dev, that girl had the face of an angel."

Lord Devaney began to splutter and protest but before he could say any more there came a knock on the door. He gave his friend an icy glance before issuing the summons to enter.

Lady Silverwood's housekeeper, a small plump lady of immaculate appearance made her entrance and bobbed a curtsey.

"Yes, Mrs Noakes?" Lord Devaney asked, having recovered his poise.

"You asked to be kept informed about the young lady, my lord ..."

Sir Hugo sat up in his chair and the other man said, "Indeed I did. Has she been made comfortable?"

"She has been put in the blue room," she answered, a trace of disapproval clearly evident in her voice, "but I am afraid she's developed a fever, my lord. Do you wish Sykes to ride for a physician?"

Lord Devaney glanced at his companion who shook his head almost imperceptibly.

"Is she so ill?"

Mrs Noakes smiled faintly. "I doubt it, my lord. I have nursed many a fever in my time but I just wanted to know your orders."

"See that she has all the care she needs

and keep Sir Hugo and myself informed of her progress. I believe that will suffice."

She inclined her head, bobbed a little curtsey and then left the room.

Smiling slightly Sir Hugo mused, "I wonder what she thinks of this matter."

"It is not a servant's place to think, Hugo, but even so no one around these parts has any love for Squire Chawton. He's a bad landlord and, from all accounts, he gives his maidservants no peace either."

"Tell me of a man who does."

The younger man looked cross again. "You have such a cynical attitude, Hugo, and I cannot conceive why. Squire Chawton is a well-known lecher and I have no reason to believe his son is any better."

"Lechery is not a crime, otherwise we shall all be clapped in jail."

"Nor is hunting young girls with a pack of hounds, but have you paused to consider what would have become of her if they'd caught her?"

The other man was considering the high shine on his boots. "They would have savaged her; that is what they are trained to do."

At that moment a footman entered, bowed low and announced, "Squire Chawton and Mr Joseph Chawton are here, my lord, and crave a few minutes of your time."

Lord Devaney gave his friend a startled look which was met with a half amused one. Recovering his composure he asked, "Shall I refuse to see them, Hugo?"

"That would only postpone the inevitable, I fear."

Lord Devaney swallowed before saying, "Very well. Show them in."

As soon as the footmen had gone he rushed over to his friend. "What to do now?" he asked in a panic-stricken voice.

"Wait until the man approaches you about the matter, but do not assume the girl an innocent victim simply because you dislike the man."

"You are determined to believe the girl guilty of some crime."

"Only because that is the likelihood."

Lord Devaney straightened up and assumed an authoritative pose in front of the fire. Sir Hugo remained where he was as the Squire and his son were ushered into the library, and he was therefore in an unparalleled position to observe them before they espied him.

The older man was short and squat, wearing a greasy wig on his bald head, filthy riding clothes and mud-splattered boots. His son was as short, but thin with light-coloured hair, not unlike straw, and pale eyes which darted everywhere, missing nothing. His pathetic efforts to ape current fashions had resulted in a vulgar display of sartorial bad taste which caused the lip of the fastidious Sir Hugo to curl.

Squire Chawton strode across the room. "Sorry to intrude, my lord, but I thought it best to warn you that a felon is on the loose."

Lord Devaney glanced uneasily to where Sir Hugo sat concealed in a high wing chair and who at that moment chose to unfurl himself to full height.

The two visitors stared at him in astonishment and with a great deal of relief evident in his voice Lord Devaney said, "Allow me to introduce Sir Hugo Lytton who is at present residing at Silverwood."

The Squire's attitude was of overt curiosity but his son stared at Sir Hugo with admiration. It was Joseph Chawton who said, "Sir Hugo, we are honoured indeed."

The baronet inclined his head stiffly in acknowledgment before asking, "A felon, you say? To warrant such a pucker he must be a murderer at the very least."

"The wench stole a purse from my son today," the Squire explained, looking a mite foolish.

"A woman!" Sir Hugo said with much surprise. "They are treacherous creatures and often far worse than their male counterparts."

The Squire looked gratified. "My pack traced her as far as the boundary of Silverwood land and then lost her by the river. We feel bound to warn you she may be in this area."

Lord Devaney continued to look both uncomfortable and anxious and it was Sir Hugo who said, "Be assured, my good fellow, if we do apprehend such a harpy we shall deliver her to the proper authorities."

"Oh, she is no harpy..."

Joseph Chawton spoke out without thinking and his father struck at him with the riding whip he had clutched in his hand, causing the young man to cringe away.

"Be silent, boy. You lusted after her so 'tis partly your fault, though," he added, addressing the two other men once more, "that is no excuse for dishonesty."

"How did the ... theft occur?" Lord Devaney ventured, adding, "if I may be so bold as to ask?"

Young Chawton stared at the floor as his father answered, "It was in the most distressing circumstances. She was a member of a band of itinerant players who gave a performance for us at the Manor. Afterwards, flouting my charity, this...doxy stole my son's purse."

Sir Hugo shook his head. "It is impossible to invite anyone into one's house nowadays with impunity."

The Squire looked mollified whereas his son continued to stare at the floor, appearing to be thoroughly chastened.

"How true, Sir Hugo. A sorry business." He eyed the madeira decanter with interest. "It is for the likes of us to keep the law. 'Tis amazing how many would break the law given the slightest opportunity." He eyed the decanter again. "We...er, perchance, should meet together to discuss such matters. There are few enough people of our class in the area..."

Sir Hugo's response to such a suggestion was to eye the man so coldly that he began to back towards the door, bowing and pulling his son with him.

"We must, regretfully, be gone for we have to call on other households to warn them to keep a watch. I am obliged to you for your time, gentlemen, and will take up no more of it."

Sir Hugo was quick to follow them to the door and even condescended to open it, smiling urbanely now. "Be assured if we can be of any assistance in upholding law and order we shall certainly do so."

Squire Chawton paused to study Sir Hugo for a moment before saying, "If you are so fortunate, sir, as to apprehend the hussy, I would be obliged if you would turn her over to *me*, as I am the magistrate for this area."

Smoothly Sir Hugo replied, "If you are the instrument of law and order be assured that we will respect your position."

Lord Devaney hurried forward then to echo his friend's assurances. When the two had gone and the door was closed behind them the younger man leaned back against it, letting out a long sigh. Then he strode across the room, slapping his friend heartily on the back and laughing in delight.

"That was famous, Hugo! You were really superb. You had those toadies ready to grease your boots. But what possessed you to protect her after all you've said?"

Sir Hugo drew out his snuff box. He flicked open the lid and took a pinch before saying in his most laconic of voices as he snapped back the lid, "Whatever her misdemeanour, her crime cannot be so great as the one young Chawton has committed with his mode of dress!"

Three

The young woman came slowly down the main staircase of Silverwood, all the while glancing about her in awe at the size and magnificence of Lady Silverwood's country home. When she reached the hall a footman opened a door for her and after staring at him uncertainly for a moment or two she went into the library.

It appeared deserted and after hesitating in the doorway she gravitated towards the fire, where she held out her hands briefly before turning to examine her surroundings in more detail.

As she turned she started uneasily to find herself being examined critically by a man who was sitting in a leather armchair which had up until that moment hidden him from her sight. As she stared at him uncertainly Sir Hugo rose slowly to his feet to tower over her and she stepped neatly to one side to put more space between them.

During the few minutes which had elapsed since her entry into the room Sir Hugo had been afforded ample opportunity to scrutinise her. Her appearance had certainly improved since he had last seen her, before delivering her into the hands of Lady Silverwood's servants.

Now her hair had been washed and was restored to its former golden glory. It was very beautiful hair, he was forced to admit to himself. He was glad to note too that the scratches on what skin was visible to him had healed although there were several fading bruises to be seen about her person. Mrs Noakes had provided her with one of Lady Silverwood's outmoded gowns and this hung loosely about her, Lady Silverwood being more rounded than this slightly built girl. He was quite amazed at the difference in her, for she looked not the least inferior, which he would expect of an intinerant player and suspected felon.

The one thing he realised had not changed about her was the fear in those round blue eyes. It was still there as she continued to stare back at him.

"Oh, you...must be Lord Devaney," she said at last in an evenly modulated voice which was understandably breathless with nervousness. "I am told you wish to see me, my lord."

"You are mistaken. I am Sir Hugo Lytton, but Lord Devaney will be here presently."

The girl bobbed a little curtsey. "I do remember you, sir. The other day..."

It was then that Lord Devaney came hurrying into the library. He paused on seeing the two already present before the door was closed behind him. He looked from one to the other rather anxiously for a moment or two before a smile came on to his face.

"My dear girl, you look so much improved since the other day. Is that not so, Hugo?"

The other man did not take his eyes from her. "I was just thinking so myself."

Two spots of colour appeared in her cheeks as she averted her eyes and curt-seyed again. "My lord, I fear my presence has been a great inconvenience to you."

"Nonsense! It is good to see you so much recovered. Is it not, Hugo?"

"Indeed." The girl eyed him uncertainly once more and he added, speaking softly, "You have the advantage of us, miss. We do not know your name."

She bit her lip before answering, "Marin Ambrose, Sir Hugo."

Lord Devaney moved a chair nearer to the fire. "You must still be weak after so severe a chill. Do sit down."

The girl smiled at him gratefully and after she was seated the other two sat down too.

"Perhaps you would be kind enough to tell us ... Miss Ambrose," Sir Hugo began, examining his nails as he spoke, "why Squire Chawton was pursuing you in so bizarre a manner."

One hand flew to her lips and her eyes filled with tears. Sir Hugo was almost moved by her distress and Lord Devaney certainly was, for he said, "Take your time, my dear. We did not wish to distress you."

Sir Hugo took out his time-piece and glanced at it momentarily before smiling blandly at the girl. "Not too much time though, Miss Ambrose, if you please."

Lord Devaney shot him a cross look and she asked, "Where am I? I have no notion ..."

"At Silverwood," Lord Devaney answered. "Which is some miles from the Manor, but the land is adjacent."

"I must have been running a long time before you found me, or at least it seemed like it."

Lord Devaney made noises of sympathy but Sir Hugo said without taking his eyes off the girl, "How did you cross the river?"

She decided she did not like his hostile manner towards her so addressed herself to the more kindly Lord Devaney. "There were some stepping stones where the water is shallow but I cannot tell you where it is."

Sir Hugo looked to his friend who nodded. "I know the place. It's about three miles from the thicket."

"Squire Chawton tells us you stole a purse from his son."

At this statement from Sir Hugo she was on her feet, ready for flight. "He knows I am here!"

Lord Devaney went to her and put his hand on her shoulder. "Now, now, my dear, there is no need to get into a pucker. Squire Chawton has no idea you are here with us so please sit down again."

He pressed her down into the chair once more and as she sat down she covered her face with her hands. "I am so sorry, but if he were to learn..."

"You stole some property ..."

At this prompting from Sir Hugo she looked up again. Her eyes were no longer full of fear; now they blazed with indignation.

"No! I stole nothing." At Sir Hugo's answering and unsympathetic stare she turned to Lord Devaney once more, looking at him pleadingly. "I swear it, my lord."

"Explain to us then what did happen," he urged, still using a gentle voice.

She sank back into the chair limply and once again covered her face with her hands. "What is the use? No one will believe *me*."

Lord Devaney gave his friend a hopeless look and Sir Hugo said, "Perhaps, but we do require to hear your side of the story before deciding on the next course of action."

She shuddered and lowered her hands to her lap. "You will hand me over to him."

"No, no, I assure you, my dear, we will not," Lord Devaney declared, sitting forward in his chair.

She looked at Sir Hugo but as he remained silent she said in a quiet voice. "I did not steal his purse."

"Then why did Mr Chawton say that you did?"

Marin Ambrose glared at Sir Hugo

resentfully. "I cannot say for certain; all I can do is tell you what did happen."

"That is precisely what I have been urging for the past ten minutes."

"I was with a band of travelling players and when we came to the Manor we offered to perform for them. All the time I was aware of his...Mr. Chawton's...scrutiny of me and I am not so green not to know what it meant. I believed they were entertained by what we did for Squire Chawton paid us well and then offered us the use of his barn for the night. It was late and we were glad enough to avail ourselves of the offer.

"At some time during the night—how long have I been here?"

"Three days," Sir Hugo informed her, still watching her carefully.

"It must have been early in the morning of the day you found me." She ran her hand through her somewhat dishevelled curls. "I have lost track of time entirely."

"It is Thursday," Lord Devaney told her.

She smiled her thanks to him and then continued with her story. "I was awakened by...Mr Chawton at my side. At first I did not realise what he was about until he began to kiss me. I began to cry out and that awoke my companions who were about to set about him. It was then ... he produced a purse and complained that I had stolen it from him. Squire Chawton was summoned and declared me his prisoner."

Sir Hugo looked uncompromisingly grim. "Are you asking us to believe that you did not steal the purse?"

Once again the girl leaped to her feet. "I shall not ask that of *you*, sir, but I vow I did not! Oh, I knew you would not believe me. Why should you? I am only an actress—a doxy with no right to a hearing. Why should you believe *my* word against that of a squire's son!".

Sir Hugo remained imperturbable whereas Lord Devaney said, "Dash it all, Hugo, young Chawton's a coxcomb if ever I saw one."

"Sit down, Miss Ambrose," Sir Hugo instructed and so severe was his tone she immediately obeyed. "Tell us why Mr Chawton would choose to lie? What he attempted to do to you is not unnatural nor unknown."

The girl blushed, her pale cheeks flooding with a colour that became her. "I did not ... know at the time, but later I came to realise he might have been afraid of the Squire."

"That is exactly my feeling," Lord Devaney declared. "That poltroon is entirely under the influence of his father and if Miss Ambrose rejected his amorous advances he would be craven enough to want revenge."

Sir Hugo stirred uneasily in his chair before taking a pinch of snuff. The girl watched him fearfully, understanding now that it was his decision which would seal her fate and not that of Lord Devaney. She watched him curiously, for she had never seen a man like him before. His distrust of her was repellent and yet she found him fascinating and supposed he epitomised the gentlemen of the *beau monde* of which she had heard so much. Certainly he was handsome in an awesome kind of way and splendidly attired. She noted gold buttons on his well-fitting coat, and gold fobs on his watch chain to which his long fingers occasionally strayed.

Before he had returned his snuff box to his pocket she asked more boldly now, "Do you intend to return me to his custody?"

Sir Hugo stroked his chin and looking at him in alarm, Lord Devaney exclaimed,

"How can we possibly do such a thing after what we know now?"

"Lord Devaney is correct, I fear," Sir Hugo answered at last and his friend beamed with delight. The girl closed her eyes momentarily in a gesture of relief even though his next utterances gave her no joy at all. "As Squire Chawton is the magistrate for this area you could not possibly expect a fair trial at his hands. The penalty for such a crime is severe, at the very least transportation to the colonies."

Marin Ambrose grew pale. "That is what Squire Chawton told me with extreme relish. I was so afraid. It would have been frightening enough had I been guilty but I was wholly innocent of the crime and that is why I ran away." Once more she shuddered at the memory.

"You are quite safe now," Lord Devaney assured her, getting up and walking to the fire. "Even if he knew of your presence here he would hesitate before challenging both Sir Hugo and myself to release you."

"Even so," Sir Hugo insisted, "you really should be tried by the law," and as he spoke her face crumpled with dismay.

"I am innocent."

"That is to be decided, and not by us."

"There would be no justice for her!" Lord Devaney protested and the girl looked to him hopefully.

"In any court Squire Chawton's word would carry over Miss Ambrose's."

Sir Hugo drew a deep sigh. "That is, alas, true and as I cannot admit any particality to the Chawtons it looks very much as if you are to be let off, Miss Ambrose. You are a very fortunate girl."

She looked away quickly unable to hold his gaze and Lord Devaney asked, "Have you been with the players for long?"

She averted her eyes. "A few weeks only."

"Forgive me for being presumptuous, but you are very young to be living such a life. What of your family?"

"None alive, my lord," she answered, giving him her attention. "My parents were poor farming folk at Derringham in Norfolk, but when they died within weeks of each other the land and cottage had to be given up to the next tenant. I had nowhere to go so made for the nearest hiring fair in the hope of finding work in a domestic capacity. It was there I met the players and they invited me to join them."

"Where are they now?"

The girl shrugged. "I cannot say. They

would not have waited for me and they could be anywhere by now."

"Would you wish to rejoin them if they could be located?"

Marin Ambrose looked away. "They would not want me. The taint of suspicion is not easily lost and as people do not trust intinerants anyway they would find me only a burden." Once more she looked at Sir Hugo who was now sitting quietly in his chair looking thoughtful. She tossed back her mass of curls before adding bitterly, "They can afford to let me go—another mouth to feed and I am not the greatest actress in the world."

Sir Hugo allowed himself a small smile. "Oh, I am certain you do yourself an injustice, Miss Ambrose."

Lord Devaney cleared his throat noisily. "We are enlightened now, but I am certain you must be quite exhausted. You really have been very ill. Perchance you would like to go back to your room and rest for a while."

With alacrity the girl got to her feet. "I am quite tired, my lord." She was just about to go when she hesitated, before asking, "Whose clothes am I wearing?"

"My sister's—Lady Elspeth Silverwood. This is her house, but she is at present in London."

"I hope she will not mind my wearing it."

Lord Devaney laughed. "She will not even recall she has it. She possesses countless gowns but only wears those of the very latest mode."

"When I have mended my own, my lord, I shall return this to Mrs Noakes."

"You must not think to do so. My sister would want you to have it."

She smiled uncertainly before bobbing a curtsey. "I am for ever indebted to you, Lord Devaney."

As she left the room he shook his head. "The injustice of if is monstrous. What chance has she of proving her innocence?"

"None," Sir Hugo answered in an uncompromising voice.

"I should like to show that coxcomb what I really think of him."

Sir Hugo was toying with a snuff box which stood on a table at the side of his chair. "Save your indignation for those who are worthy of it, Dev."

"How right you are." He grinned gleefully then. "But I cannot quarrel with

young Chawton's taste on this occasion.
You must admit, she is an uncommonly
fetching chit."

Still toying with the box Sir Hugo replied
thoughtfully, "Fetching perhaps in a rustic
way, but not uncommonly so."

Lord Devaney's eyebrows rose a fraction.
"Well, I cannot confess to *your* experience of
females."

The other man smiled at what was
intended as a compliment and then asked,
"When she is fully recovered you will have
to send her on her way."

"Lord no! Can't do that, Hugo. She'd be in
trouble again in no time. With her looks and
innocence she'd be natural prey to the next
rogue she came across, and perchance not
so lucky on that occasion."

"Mayhap you should ask Lady Silverwood if she wishes to have a permanent
guest at Silverwood."

Lord Devaney was taken aback. "What
can be done with her?"

Sir Hugo smiled. "Ah, at last you comprehend the difficulty."

"I know the answer!" the young man
cried then, ignoring his friend's heavy
sarcasm. "She can *work* here. There is
always a need for kitchen maids, and as the

intinerant way of life has disenchanted her I am certain the girl will be glad of the opportunity to turn her hand to proper work."

He looked to his friend for confirmation of the idea but Sir Hugo only drew a deep sigh before reaching for the decanter.

Four

"I must confess," Lord Devaney confided, looking up from the book in which he had until then been immersed, "that rusticating hasn't been as dull as I'd feared."

Sir Hugo had been standing by the drawing room window, gazing out, but now he turned to smile at his friend. "It has not been without incident."

His friend chuckled. "Indeed not. I would not have missed that little to-do for all the routs and card parties in London. Hugo, all Elspeth's outstanding matters of business have been settled and I must say I feel satisfied to have settled that child into honest work here."

"She was most reluctant to accept the offer of work, which is odd, for you seemed convinced she would be only too pleased."

"Oh, no doubt she believed me inventing the need for a kitchen maid and didn't wish to be further indebted, but she realised, naturally, it would be foolhardy for her to venture forth into the world alone and unprotected."

"Many women do."

Lord Devaney gazed unseeingly across the room. "They are invariably lowly creatures. This one is different."

"I am inclined to agree with you there," Sir Hugo said with heavy irony which his friend did not seem to grasp.

He looked at him with interest. "So you too have noted it?"

"Indeed."

Sir Hugo transferred his attention to the garden once more. "She has a rare quality about her for a maid of her station," Lord Devaney murmured before returning his interest to the volume on his knee. "She has a delicacy of manner rare in a farm labourer's daughter."

"You have had little experience of farm labourer's daughters," Sir Hugo pointed out.

His friend laughed. "It may be that we have missed an experience, Hugo!"

Sir Hugo frowned suddenly as he gazed out at the tranquil countryside all around and then he stiffened. A moment later he turned on his heel and strode across the room, much to the other man's surprise.

"Hugo, what is amiss?"

"Nothing which needs concern you; there is a matter I must needs attend to without delay," he told Lord Devaney before rushing out of the room.

He hurried out of the house and then ran swiftly through the gardens to the orchard and beyond it where the fields began. There he paused to look about him, his hands on his hips. Suddenly he caught sight of his quarry running ahead of him and he set off in pursuit once more. It took him very little time to catch up with her. Just as he was a few yards away she realised he was there and after glancing back she tried to run faster, not knowing she had no chance of outpacing him.

Her eyes widened with fear and he called "Stop! Stop, I say."

Her reply was to make a dash to escape him. He reached out to catch hold of her arm but it was only fleetingly for she managed to tear herself free of him and run on. Only a few yards further on he succeeded in catching up with her once more but as he snatched at her arm she stumbled in the long grass, dragging him to the ground with her which caused him to curse roundly.

Even with some of the wind knocked out

of her she still managed to struggle although it was an unequal one. Although he was just as breathless as she, Sir Hugo had little hardship holding her down, for she was slight of build, a mere slip of a girl.

"Let me go!" she cried, turning this way and that in her efforts to be free of his grip.

"Not until you tell me what you've done."

"Nothing! I vow I have done nothing."

"Then why are you running away?"

"Oh, please let me go, Sir Hugo. Just let me go."

"Not until I discover what you have stolen from Silverwood House."

Realising the inequality of her struggle she resisted no longer and lay quiet whilst he held her hands above her head and towered over her.

"Come now, admit to it before I am forced to search you to find out for myself. What is it? A piece of silver? A snuff box?"

Her eyes blazed into his. "You are a vile and abominable man! How dare you make such unwarranted accusations?"

"Unwarranted are they? Why *are* you running away?"

"You still believe me a thief. I knew it all the time! You are as bad as Joseph Chawton. Worse. He does not put on the airs of a gentleman. He knows precisely what he is but you are a vile, vile man."

"Shame on you," he scoffed. "How can you be so unjust after I ruined a good coat by wrapping you in it? Now, do you tell me or do I find out for myself?"

She began to struggle anew but to no avail and realising it at last tears began to stream down her face.

"I have stolen nothing. Nothing. I just could...not bear it in that kitchen any longer. It was unbearable, scrubbing, cleaning, fetching, carrying. Cook beat me with a broom this morning."

"Why?" he demanded, making no attempt to hide his amusement.

Marin Ambrose continued to sob. "I spilled the soup all over the kitchen floor. Oh, I will *not* be a kitchen maid any longer."

He smiled openly now, still not letting his grip on her loosen one iota. "Are you not accustomed to menial work on the farm, Miss Ambrose? Is it too lowly an occupation for a farm labourer's daughter?" Her eyes grew wilder and he said, losing none of his calm, "Why don't you tell me where you really come from?"

"I don't know what you may mean. I have already told you all there is to know."

"But not the truth, I'll warrant. One thing I am convinced about, you are no farm labourer's daughter."

"But I am. Why will you persist in not believing me?"

"Be assured I have known all the ways and wiles of females and it is very clear to me that not one word of your explanation to Lord Devaney and myself is true. You speak too well to be what you say, and you have an air about you no rustic could possibly possess. I mean to know, Miss Ambrose," he added threateningly.

The tears began to flow again and he looked at her askance. "Oh, Miss Ambrose, such a ploy does not become you. I am not a man to be moved by tears."

"Nothing, I am persuaded, would move *you*, Sir Hugo."

Suddenly he looked up in alarm, becoming aware of the approach of a horseman. "Hell's teeth!" he cried. "Squire Chawton."

"Oh no!" she cried. "What am I to do? If only you had let me go when I begged you. Now I am lost, lost!"

"Let us have none of the vapours, miss! Get up and keep quiet," he ordered, letting her wrists go at last.

He scrambled to his feet, brushing the

dust off his normally immaculate breeches. Then, when she remained on the ground he stooped to pull her to her feet and once more kept a tight grip on her wrist. This was accomplished just as Squire Chawton reached them on his hack. Without troubling to dismount he pointed one stubby finger at the girl who made no attempt to free herself any more. Fear, it seemed, had transfixed her.

"You've apprehended her at last! Well done, Sir Hugo. You have my admiration and thanks."

The younger man regarded him stonily. "I beg your pardon, sir; are you by any chance referring to this lady?"

"You must know I am. This is the wench who stole Joseph's purse."

Sir Hugo laughed. "You are sadly mistaken sir. I recall that you made some mention of an escaped felon but this lady happens to be a relative of the late Lord Silverwood and is presently visiting Lady Silverwood." He looked at Marin and laughed. "The wench who stole a purse, indeed! What Lady Silverwood would say to that I cannot imagine."

The man's jaw dropped and Sir Hugo sensed that the girl's tension had eased a little. "You were struggling to apprehend her, I am sure of it."

"How dare you assume we should be so undignified," Sir Hugo replied in his iciest tone. "We were out walking when Miss Ambrose stumbled and fell. What you perceived were my efforts to help her to her feet."

"But my eyes cannot deceive me so. I could have sworn..."

"Enough, Squire Chawton. I find your attitude insulting. The lady would appreciate an apology I am certain."

The man although obviously perplexed bowed low in the saddle. "I meant no disrespect, ma'am, only you look uncommonly like an escaped felon we are seeking."

In a manner quite different to that she had so far displayed Marin Ambrose drew herself up to full height. "I, a *felon*! Who *is* this impertinent fellow, Hugo?" she demanded, tossing back her head haughtily. "I declare I do not like the look of him."

"No one of any consequence, my dear," Sir Hugo replied without taking his eyes off the Squire who had grown rather red of face.

Warming to the role Marin went on to

say, "Has not Lady Silverwood's game-keeper been given orders to shoot on sight any trespasser?"

"Indeed he has, for we are plagued with poachers. Have a care, Squire Chawton, when you leave the estate lest you are mistaken for one."

Turning his horse the Squire dug in his heels and galloped away, leaving Sir Hugo to stare after him, a small smile playing at the corners of his mouth. When she murmured, "Thank you, Sir Hugo," in a soft voice he looked at her once more and she asked, rather uneasily, "Do you think he was convinced?"

Sir Hugo's eyes remained on the retreating figure of the squire. "No," he answered, "even though your performance was an excellent one. He is a little perplexed but I fear he will be back when he has had time to ponder on the matter. He has right on his side."

He turned to look at her at last in time to see the fear return to her eyes, but it gave him no satisfaction.

"What shall I do? Oh, you must see you have to let me go now. I must leave this place immediately."

"On foot, on your own? A chit of your

tender years will soon be in trouble again. You have no notion as to the ugliness in the minds of men."

Her lips curled into a sneer of derision. "I am certain you know a deal about such matters, Sir Hugo. I would as leif take a chance on the outside world as with you."

"On two occasions I protected you from Squire Chawton," he pointed out. "I wonder what your opinion of me would have been had I let you go."

She bit her lip uncertainly. "You have done me a service, I readily admit it although I am puzzled as to why for you certainly do not trust me." When he made no reply and only regarded her in a mocking way which disconcerted her she asked, "Do you intend to let me go? There is no longer any cause for you or Lord Devaney to shelter me."

"I am still much too curious about you to let you go so easily. One thing is certain, though; you cannot remain here in safety but whether you go to a safe place or to face your accusers after all is dependent on your ability to tell the truth."

She averted her eyes and when he said, "Come with me," she did not demur; she knew it would be useless to do so.

They did not return immediately to the house. Instead he led her to an arbour hidden by privets and bushes where he seated her on a bench. Standing four-square in front of her he folded his arms and said, "Lord Devaney is in many ways an innocent where scheming females are concerned and I am rather too fond of him to allow his hospitality to be abused by one."

Marin looked up at his uncompromising countenance and her lips trembled mutinously. "If you recall, Sir Hugo, I did not choose to partake of Lord Devaney's hospitality."

"My dear girl, you were in no condition to decide for yourself. Had we left you you might well have died of fever if the hounds hadn't torn you to pieces first." She lowered her eyes once more and he went on, "Miss Ambrose, you have prevaricated long enough. I can even now call the magistrate, so do not think to gammon me any longer."

Her head snapped up, her eyes sparkling with defiance. "I had no wish to deceive Lord Devaney—or anyone else. I ... thought it best not to tell all the truth. I have my reasons."

"Which we will discuss in due course, but in the meantime let us begin with your name. Marin Ambrose sounds too much like an actress's name to be real."

The girl drew herself up straight. "I assure you it is my real name."

His lips curved into the semblance of a smile. "Recall, I shall know if you lie to me. You may consider yourself very clever, but I am no stupid clodpole."

"You are far, far worse, Sir Hugo."

Unfolding his arms he drew a deep sigh. "It appears you will have to be questioned by those better equipped than I to do so."

Just as he was about to turn away she said quickly, "My name really is Prudence. Prudence Marin Ambrose. Prudence is a name I have always hated and therefore I took the earliest opportunity to discard it. The truth, Sir Hugo, is not so different to what I told you, and certainly has no bearing on anything that has happened to me since I left home. It is merely that I have no wish for my relatives to discover me."

"I am aware of that."

When he sat down on a low wall she began to feel less intimidated by him and keeping her eyes averted she continued, "My late father was a preacher. He called himself a man of God but he was nothing of the kind; just the type of man who preaches hell-fire and damnation. In his eyes all men are sinners and life must be one of eternal penance. My mother died soon after I was born and my elder sister, who is some years older than I, brought me up, but it was a hard life, how hard I am only just beginning to discover." Uncertainly she raised her eyes to his. "When I was at home I thought everyone must live as we did. It was only as I grew older that I began to suspect they did not."

"You were obviously very poor."

"It was not poverty. Mama and Papa both had inheritances; you see, Papa came late to his calling, some time after he was married. It was his beliefs which caused the hardship. There was no comfort in our home. Cold water to wash in and no fires even in the depths of winter. Needless to add, laughter was frowned upon as was music and singing. As I grew older I began to question that God really intended us to behave in such a manner but whenever I mentioned it to Papa I was beaten for my wickedness."

"Did your sister feel as you did?" he asked, revealing no sign whether he believed her or not.

Marin shook her head. "Charity is as

devout as Papa and shares his beliefs, but," she added with a sigh, "I am fond of her and always will be."

"Yet you ran away from home..."

"Papa was even harder on me after Charity married and left home, for he suspected I had wicked thoughts, but however much he punished me I could not view life as he did. After Papa died Charity and her husband gave me a home with them. I was happier for a while even though my brother-in-law was little better than Papa. Then one day Charity told me that Henry—her husband—had made a match for me." Her hands clenched with emotion. "She did not believe I should have any say in the matter as it had all been decided. Papa had chosen *her* husband and she had been glad enough to comply so she could not conceive why I should not wish to, even though he was a man I detested which was in itself considered wicked. He was a decent, God-fearing man and that was all which mattered.

"I was desperate—I knew I could not marry him and continue to live my life in such a manner, but I was also very sure if I remained at their home I *would* submit to pressure and marry him, and then there would never be any escape. It was then that I decided to seek another life. It was not an easy decision to take but I was aware there had to be something better."

"Did you find something better with the actors?"

She sighed. "No, for it was not as I thought it would be. In many of the places we visited people did not want us. Several times we went hungry and had no fit place in which to sleep. It occurred to me that I had merely exchanged one dreadful existence for another."

"How did you come to join them?" he asked, his eyes narrowing thoughtfully.

"They just happened to be in the area of my sister's home. I saw them in the market place one day when I was shopping with Charity. If she had known I was watching them she would have been very angry, but whilst she was intent upon her shopping I contrived to evade her for a while. What I saw was a whole new world; people who laughed, danced, sang and wore pretty clothes. One of the players who came into the audience to collect money recognised my interest and spoke to me. I told her I would like to be an actress and she invited me to join them.

"That night I crept out of the house and we were on the road before my sister would have missed me. That, Sir Hugo, is my story but I beg of you not to tell my sister where I am. I would kill myself rather than go back now I have tasted the fruits of freedom."

"No one will force you to go back, but you are an innocent alone in what you have discovered to be a very wicked world, so is there no other relative with whom you could seek refuge?"

She shook her head again. "Because of his extreme views Papa had lost contact with both his and Mama's relatives long before I was born. I had a brother whom I can scarce remember, for he was already grown when I was born. I came to my parents late in their lives. My brother could not bear so harsh a life and did not want to become a preacher as my father intended, so he ran away from home too, but that was many years ago. As I said, he is only a vague memory to me."

"You have not heard of him since?"

"Papa disowned him entirely. The matter was never spoken of but from what I discovered elsewhere I believe he joined the army, for that is what he always wanted to do. That was another reason why I liked the idea of travelling with the actors; at each town I enquired for my brother, but in truth I believe him long dead."

Sir Hugo stood up at last and she looked at him fearfully. "The most pressing need now is to remove you from here before Squire Chawton returns. You really have been the most foolhardy creature."

Getting to her feet also Marin murmured, "I realise it now but I could not for anything remain and marry Jacob Fletcher. He was old—at least thirty—and was for ever reading me a sermon. He was not in the least handsome either."

"Would it have made any difference if he were?" Sir Hugo asked politely.

"I think not."

Sir Hugo smiled slightly. "You must tell your story to Lord Devaney now and then we must make haste to depart."

"He will be most terribly angry," she said as she followed him back towards the house.

"You have no cause to fear his wrath, but," he added darkly, "you will need to fear mine if you have been anything but open with me."

He paused as they were about to enter the house and she looked up at him, never doubting that he did indeed mean what he said.

Five

When Marin Ambrose, escorted by Sir Hugo, entered the drawing room it was to find Lord Devaney and Mrs Noakes in earnest conversation together. The moment the other two entered the room the conversation ceased abruptly.

"Where have you been you naughty girl?" Mrs Noakes cried, and then, looking at Sir Hugo, "I am sorry you have been troubled, sir, but be assured I will deal with her now."

As the housekeeper came towards her, Marin automatically shrank back but Sir Hugo said, "I have been made aware of the altercation in the kitchen and the matter has been attended to, Mrs Noakes. Miss Ambrose regrets any inconvenience she has caused to you and Cook." He hesitated before adding, "She will be leaving here today so there will be no more...trouble."

The housekeeper looked about to say more but thought better of it. Instead she bobbed a curtsey and left the room, her lips stretched to a thin line of disapproval.

The moment she had done so Lord Devaney asked, "What the devil is going on? Mrs Noakes told me the girl had run off." He viewed her with uncharacteristic severity. "Cook has found you totally disobedient, Miss Ambrose."

Sir Hugo walked into the centre of the room leaving Marin by the door. He seemed to dominate the room with his presence and when he glanced back at Marin he smiled faintly.

"Miss Ambrose finds menial work beneath her dignity, Dev."

Lord Devaney glared at the girl. "Does she indeed?"

"It is evident to me she will never make a satisfactory servant. When she has explained some matters to you, I believe you will agree with me."

Marin Ambrose stepped forward. "Lord Devaney, I have deceived you and must beg your pardon most heartily."

He looked at her more curiously then and she went on to tell him all she had previously revealed to Sir Hugo. He walked across to the window and with his back to

the room stared out into the distance all the
while she was speaking. When she had
finished and had lapsed into an embarrassed silence he turned around again.

Lord Devaney looked from one to the
other and then began to laugh. "It wasn't
such a great sin after all." He glanced at Sir
Hugo. "I always thought she was too
top-lofty to be a rustic."

Sir Hugo smiled to himself before saying,
"She will have to leave here, Dev. The
Squire has seen us together and although
we have perhaps allayed his suspicions it is
likely he will be back."

The viscount's face fell. "Yes, indeed. We
must remove her from danger ..."

Sir Hugo gave her a long look before
saying, "Go along and collect your belongings, Miss Ambrose. We shall leave Silverwood within the hour."

"Where shall you be taking me?"

"That is something yet to be decided. Go
along, girl, and be ready when you are
summoned."

Marin Ambrose looked about to say more
but then after curtseying to them both went
out of the room. Lord Devaney watched her
go before immediately turning to his friend.

"It is all very well your saying she must be removed but where can she go? What are we to do with her?"

The other man laughed. "I did warn you of possible problems. You cannot take up a girl and then abdicate responsibility."

"Dash it all, Hugo, we could not have allowed a girl of her kind to be hunted like an animal. She is an innocent and a maiden of quality."

"You did not know that at the time," Sir Hugo pointed out.

"Oh, does it matter?" he answered bad temperedly. "One must admire her bravery after leading such a sheltered life. Her background is incredible. I never imagined anyone could live in such a manner."

Sir Hugo walked purposefully towards the door. "I am going to order my carriage. I think we should take her to London where she will be safe—at least from Chawton."

Viscount Devaney began to pace to and fro. "I assume we cannot let her loose on the Town. She would be picked up by some bawdy house madam within minutes of her arrival. We shall have to place her in some respectable household."

"Do you know of one which would be suitable?"

Lord Devaney's eyes suddenly lit up with excitement. "We'll take her to Elspeth's place! *She* can take care of her!"

At this suggestion Sir Hugo threw back his head and laughed. "I can scarce imagine Lady Silverwood as hostess to someone as green as Miss Ambrose."

The younger man stiffened with indignation. "She is a perfectly respectable female from good family, Hugo, as you have already observed."

"But nevertheless not quite your sister's style."

Lord Devaney continued to look indignant. "The girl is homeless without friend or kin. Truth to tell, Hugo, I feel responsible for her," he averted his eyes, "in a brotherly way, naturally."

"Naturally," his friend answered sarcastically. "What would Lady Silverwood do with her? She could scarce introduce her to her own circle of acquaintances."

"I cannot conceive why not," the other man protested and then he frowned slightly. "It would answer if we could find her a husband."

"Her sister's attempt to do just that resulted in her running away."

"Oh, not some canting puritan. A good

man with whom she can fall in love in the most natural way."

Sir Hugo looked unbelieving. "She will not find anyone of that description in your sister's circle."

"Why not? She is exceedingly fair of face with a comely figure and a submissive nature. She could outshine any of this Season's hopefulls."

"That is not to say a great deal. However, with such a robust opinion as to her qualities I only wonder you do not offer for her yourself. You would make a handsome pair, and such children resulting from your union are bound to be bonny."

The young man's cheeks grew red. "Oh, do stop jesting, Hugo. You know full well when I wed it must needs be to a chit with a fair portion. Would that I was in a position to consider her. With fine clothes she could take the *ton* by a storm."

Sir Hugo shook his head. "I fear that once again your fancies have run amok, my friend. She is but a simple preacher's daughter, a green girl, not a Society miss."

"A matter only of the appropriate apparel. She has the manner. Elspeth can present her. What would follow is only natural."

"It cannot be done unless you wish to present her in Dublin to Irish Society."

Lord Devaney laughed. "You still do not believe I am serious about this. I think she could be presented in London. She is fair enough to win hearts in London."

"Never. You'd have more success trying to put a hat upon a hen."

Lord Devaney's eyes were aglow once more. "Very well then, if you insist upon scoffing I shall wager a thousand guineas that it can be done."

Sir Hugo's eyes narrowed. "A wager?"

"Why not? There have been odder ones recorded."

"Of all the cork-brained schemes ... you cannot be serious."

"But I am, and by the end of the Season I shall be a thousand guineas richer."

Sir Hugo shook his head. "No, Dev, I shall not take up such a wager."

"You must. You really did challenge me so you are honour bound."

"I have wagered upon many a strange sport, but none so odd as this. It is fraught with difficulty."

"How so? Elspeth can present her—as one of Silverwood's distant relatives. There are many bucks who would be entranced by her beauty and innocence and have no need to dangle after a fortune. The fact that she has no fortune must weigh the odds in your favour," he added slyly.

Sir Hugo was still not convinced. "How can we persuade her to cooperate with us?"

"Naturally we cannot tell her about the wager. That would spoil everything and it cannot be recorded in a wager's book at any of our clubs, but given the chance of a London Season she will jump at it. She did, after all, leave home in search of a more ... exciting life."

Sir Hugo nodded at last. "Very well. We cannot abandon her now and I dare say no harm can come of a small wager. I rarely have the opportunity to win a thousand guineas with such ease." He flicked a minute fleck of dust from the sleeve of his coat before opening the door. "And now we must make ready to leave. I only hope Lady Silverwood is as enthusiastic as you, for on her shoulders will fall the most onerous part of this wager."

"Elspeth is a great girl. She herself enjoys gambling and she will delight in the novelty of this, I know it."

Sir Hugo studied him carefully for a moment or two. "There is just one condition,

Dev; no pressure must be put on the girl to marry anyone. If the opportunity arises the decision must be hers."

He grinned. "I am not such a coxcomb, Hugo. That chit is not one to be pressured into anything, but she is avid for romance. After the life she has led and the man chosen for her by the family, I am persuaded she will wish to marry the first buck who asks for her hand."

Sir Hugo did not answer; he merely gave his friend one last disbelieving look before making his exit.

"Charles, my dear, how nice it is to see you back in London again. The Town has been much too quiet without you."

Lady Silverwood rose from her seat and came towards her brother. He took her hand and kissed it, and after he had let it go she transferred her attention to Sir Hugo. The moment her eyes alighted on him they grew moist and her voice softened considerably as she addressed him.

"Hugo, I am so pleased you have come too. We do not see you nearly often enough, and it was kind of you to bear Charles company."

He too raised her hand to his lips and

after he had let it go again she seemed reluctant to move away. However, after a moment or two she did so, her skirts rustling as she moved towards a sofa.

"Come and sit down and tell me when you returned from Silverwood."

"We came directly here," her brother replied.

Her cheeks flushed with pleasure. "I am indeed honoured. Was rusticating so *very* boring?"

Lord Devaney chuckled. "It was far from that, Elspeth."

At this admission she looked taken aback. "That from you, Charles, is a strange statement." She glanced sideways at Sir Hugo. "I am persuaded *you* must have found it a trial, Hugo."

"As you are about to learn, Lady Silverwood, the visit proved to be a most diverting interlude."

Lady Silverwood continued to look bewildered and her brother asked quickly, "How is Remington faring? Have you heard?"

"Remington! La! He is quite recovered—at least from his injury. His dear Mama was intent upon taking action against you—as you suspected she would—until it was pointed out that her son was as much to blame in the eyes of the law." She began to chuckle. "She was so frightened she took him off to France on the first packet boat and they have not returned yet!"

The two men laughed also and after a minute or two Lady Silverwood considered them thoughtfully, tapping her fan against her lips. "There is an air about you both which intrigues me. What did you mean about the visit to Silverwood being diverting? Truth to tell I looked to see you back a se'ennight ago and yet you seem content enough to have stayed."

Lord Devaney glanced meaningfully at his friend. "Perhaps Hugo had better explain..."

Lady Silverwood tapped him on the knee with her fan. "Yes, do explain. I'm in quite a fever to know."

Sir Hugo took a leisurely pinch of snuff between his finger and thumb, inhaling it before he recounted the story of Marin Ambrose, during which time she grew more and more astonished.

When he had finished she began to laugh. "You are incorrigible. A wager indeed. The poor creature. You should be ashamed of yourselves for using her so ill."

Lord Devaney pointed out quickly, "Not as ill as Squire Chawton would have used her, Elspeth."

"The man is an abomination, 'tis true."

"Do you not know," Sir Hugo remarked, "your brother will wager upon anything?"

Smiling wryly, she nodded. "Indeed I do. When I made my debut did he not wager upon which of my suitors I would choose? And when I was increasing he wagered not upon what sex the child would be but on the colour of her hair. But then, dear Hugo," she added in a sweet tone, "you have never failed to take him up on any of them."

"Well, there is a practical side to this one. We had no notion what to do with the chit, but if you feel unable to chaperon her the wager must needs be called off."

She gave Sir Hugo a coquettish look. "What kind of a person would I be to refuse to help my own brother? A thousand guineas is not to be scorned."

"Assuming that Dev wins ..."

"How can he lose?" Her face took on a sudden look of dismay. "Of course I have yet to see her! She is not hag-faced, is she?"

"By no stretch of the imagination," her brother assured her and she relaxed once more, her thoughts quite obviously milling around in her head. "Ask Hugo. He is a fair judge of the female countenance."

She glanced at him and he said indolently, "She is fair enough to turn some poor fellow's head, I dare say."

"Do *you* find her fetching?"

"She is but a child. My fancy usually leads me to ladies of a more mature kind. All I will admit is that she has a faint chance of attracting some callow youth. It was not I who called the wager; I have merely taken it up."

Lady Silverwood tapped her fan thoughtfully against the back of her hand. "Does she possess anything of her own?"

"Nothing," her brother replied, "save your discarded gowns which Mrs Noakes found for her."

"Then she will need some items of clothing."

"Send me the vouchers," her brother urged as Sir Hugo sat back on the sofa.

"There will be only a few purchases necessary, I fancy. Some of my own gowns—and Caroline's perhaps—can be adapted for her use. What are her accomplishments? Can she sing, dance, play an instrument? I assume she can read and write."

Lord Devaney looked at Sir Hugo in dismay before answering, "We do not know."

"Then when can I see her for myself?"

Sir Hugo unfurled himself from his comfortable seat. "Immediately. She is waiting just beyond that door."

Lady Silverwood jumped to her feet. "This is famous! I cannot wait to begin. It is the most diverting thing I have known for years, and just when the Season has become wearing. You did say she has no relatives apart from the abominable sister?"

Sir Hugo had been halfway across the room but he paused now. "She did make mention of a brother who also had the good sense to run away from home many years ago. Miss Ambrose suspects that he joined the army and it is like that he was killed in action."

Lady Silverwood's eyes narrowed thoughtfully. "That is an odd coincidence, for I had a gallant some two or three years ago by the name of Ambrose; Captain Matthew Ambrose. He was a member of Watier's. A splendidly entertaining fellow and I cannot for the moment recall why he stopped calling on me." She looked at Sir Gugo. "I hardly think there can be a connection, for this fellow was no end of a rake, a deep gambler too. I haven't seen him in a twelvemonth, perhaps even longer."

"It is a possibility, however remote, and I will certainly make some enquiries at Watiers," Sir Hugo agreed, "but in the meantime shall I show her in?"

Lady Silverwood's eyes gleamed with pleasurable anticipation. "Oh, please do, Hugo. I cannot wait to see her! The remainder of this Season is going to be a joy to anticipate!"

Six

Marin Ambrose could not stop peering all around her in awe. She was seated on a brocade sofa outside Lady Silverwood's drawing room and never in her life had she seen such magnificence. Used to spartan surroundings she could not even begin to imagine that anyone lived in ease such as this. Even the country house from which they had come was not as imposing as this.

Elegant furniture was everywhere, walls of marble and mouldings of gold leaf adorned every wall, and liveried flunkies were legion.

Ever since Sir Hugo's elegant town carriage rumbled into the centre of London, Marin had scarcely been able to contain her excitement. Everywhere she had looked exquisitely dressed people strolled, wearing clothes she had been taught to look upon as the heights of immodesty. All the time she peered wide-eyed from the carriage window, she had been aware of Sir Hugo's eyes upon her, something she found profoundly disconcerting. With Lord Devaney she was only slightly uncomfortable, but Sir Hugo invariably caused her emotions to become tumultuous at the slightest glance. At one and the same time he frightened and fascinated her. Was he as wicked as he seemed? she wondered. She could not be certain, for he hadn't betrayed her to Squire Chawton.

The world at large really was a dangerous place and she had little cause to trust these people any more than the Squire and his son, but somehow she had managed to enter their exclusive world, which was far more than she ever dared to expect. Marin drew a sigh, knowing that for however long the dream lasted she must try to derive as much pleasure out of it as possible.

Once more she averted her mind from more disturbing thoughts and instead returned her mind to the exciting images of the city she had seen on her way to Lady Silverwood's Park Lane mansion. It was very much as she had pictured from the novels she had read in secret beneath the bedcovers by the light of a single candle. So far novels had been her only link with a more indulgent world than the one she had always known, and she supposed that was why they were looked upon as wicked. Without them she might never have come to learn that there were people who did not regard pleasure as a sin. Quite the contrary; it was apparent that these people regarded the pursuit of pleasure almost as a religion.

The drawing room door clicked open and she started as Sir Hugo came out. He towered over her as she sat on the sofa playing with the strings of her bonnet.

"Lady Silverwood will receive you now, Miss Ambrose."

Marin's heart was beating fast as she entered the drawing room. She saw first the blazing fire, a phenomenon which seemed strange on such a clement day. From the fire she gazed around until she saw Lady Silverwood. Gowned in blue silk with a gauze neckerchief about her breast Lady Silverwood did look imposing but Marin caught her breath, for she had never seen such a beautiful woman. Her face was lightly painted, two small patches adorned her cheeks, and her red hair was dressed in a mass of powdered curls which framed her features prettily.

Realising she had been staring rudely, Marin dropped into a deep curtsey whereupon Lady Silverwood stepped forward and drew her to her feet.

Looking rather amused she said, "I had forgotten I possessed such a gown."

"Lord Devaney said you would not mind," Marin managed to stammer.

"That is perfectly true, especially as it becomes you far better than me. You are a very pretty child."

Marin blushed with embarrassment and without taking her eyes off the newcomer Lady Silverwood said, "Charles, I do believe you have a winner here."

Marin realised that the three were staring at her in a way which she found both perplexing and uncomfortable. She averted her eyes as Lady Silverwood moved away. "Would you care to stay here with me, Miss Ambrose?"

Marin looked up sharply. "It would be an honour, Lady Silverwood, to serve you."

The woman laughed delightedly. "I did not quite mean that, my dear. I lead an active social life, so ... are you able to sing or dance?" She turned and smiled at Marin once more. "I shall call you Marin, if I may. It is such a pretty name."

The girl flushed with pleasure. "I should be honoured, my lady. I ... am told I possess a pleasant voice. I do not know if Lord Devaney told you of my background..."

Lady Silverwood clucked her tongue. "Lamentable."

"Because of it I learned nothing of music, but whilst I was with the players they taught me to dance and to sing a little."

Lady Silverwood waved her hand in the air. "It is of no matter. My daughter's dancing master will give you some lessons."

Marin's eyes gleamed. "I should like that."

"It will be advisable," Sir Hugo suggested, "if it is generally assumed you *are* one of the late Lord Silverwood's relatives lest your family come to hear of your presence. I fancy they would not approve."

Marin grinned. "They would not indeed, but will not his other relatives know me as a stranger?"

"My late husband has few relatives still living. You will be accepted more readily as such, my dear."

"I cannot conceive why you should be so kind to me," Marin said, looking troubled, "and I cannot impose upon you. Lord Devaney and Sir Hugo have done so much for me already. I think it may be best if I went my own way."

Lady Silverwood clucked her tongue once more. "Nonsense. You are a very pleasing child and will cause quite a stir. It will be my pleasure and," she added craftily, "you will serve as a companion to me. I am long widowed and often lonely," she added wistfully, and Sir Hugo averted his face to hide a wry smile.

Marin's eyes grew wide. "You, my lady! But someone as beautiful as you..."

"Alas, 'tis true though. I will welcome your presence in my house, and after escaping your own...joyless background you will be enabled to enjoy a little of the pleasures London has to offer."

"Oh, my lady, it would be wonderful. Even now I feel I must be dreaming."

Lord Devaney looked at his friend with satisfaction whilst Lady Silverwood gave them both triumphant smiles.

The bedchamber was as opulently appointed as the rest of the house. Marin was tired after so eventful a day but even so she knew she would not be able to sleep for excitement. Outside her window there was a continuous commotion. Carriages rattled by endlessly, people shouted and laughed and street hawkers called out their wares as they passed. She peered out of the window watching the activity for some considerable time until with a sigh of pleasure she returned her attention to the room.

She felt dusty after so long a time on the road and having a wash was now a priority. The water she found waiting in the washstand was softly scented and actually warm. This was a marvel she had enjoyed at Silverwood but it still seemed strange to her. Marin washed slowly to make the most of such an unaccustomed luxury, for she still could scarcely believe her good fortune. It all seemed far too fortuitous to be true.

After she had finished washing she began to explore her room, starting with the half tester bed draped with puce satin which she could not help but touch reverently several times, so beautiful did the material feel against her skin. She was just testing the incredible softness of the mattress when there came a knock at the door.

Startled she looked up to see a girl of about thirteen or fourteen peer around the door. When she caught sight of Marin she came further into the room.

"May I come in?"

"It looks as though you are in."

The girl grinned. "My name is Caroline. I am Lady Silverwood's daughter."

Marin scrambled off the bed. "I am very pleased to meet you, but Lady Silverwood does not look old enough to have a grown-up daughter."

"You must tell that to Mama. She will be very pleased. Everyone thinks her to be a mere girl until they see me."

"That is hardly surprising, for she is very beautiful."

The girl stood very straight. "I have overheard people remark that by the time I make my debut I shall be even more beautiful."

"You should not listen in to what people say, Caroline. I am certain your Mama would never countenance such a thing."

The girl drew a deep sigh. "I did hope you would be an amusing companion, but I fear you are as prosy as the others. Listening in to conversations is my only diversion since I am still in the schoolroom. It is amazing what secrets I learn. I can tell you a great deal..."

"Oh no. Please don't. I don't want to hear."

Caroline shrugged her shoulders. Even at

such a tender age she displayed a little of the beauty she had inherited from her mother.

"Are you Lady Silverwood's only child?" Marin ventured.

"I am afraid so. Papa died not long after I was born."

"That is a pity."

She looked at Marin appraisingly. "I was not aware there were any more Silverwood relatives I had not already met. I wonder why we have not seen each other before."

"Oh, it is a very distant connection," Marin answered hastily, aware that this child was exceptionally perceptive.

"You came with Sir Hugo and Uncle Charles from Silverwood, did you not?"

The girl was looking at her curiously and Marin said, "They have been very kind to me."

"What do you think of Sir Hugo?" Caroline asked in a sly way which startled Marin somewhat.

"Why . . . he is a very fine gentleman."

"Mama hopes to marry him one day. I heard her talking about it to her maid once."

"Oh . . . I had no idea, but they do appear a handsome couple."

"That is what everyone says, but I hope they do not marry."

"Why? It seems an eminently suitable match."

"I shall make my debut in less than three years and he is the only man I would want to marry."

Marin bit back a laugh. "But he is so much older than you."

"My own Papa was more than twenty years older than Mama."

Marin could think of nothing more to say and the girl went on in a bright voice, "I am certain Sir Hugo will prefer me when I am just a little older; after all Mama is so old now."

At this Marin could not stifle her laughter. "She is the most beautiful woman I have ever seen, Caroline."

"She has had many lovers since Papa died and I do not think Sir Hugo likes that. From what I have observed he is the kind of man who prefers his mistresses to concern themselves only with him—until he tires of *them*. Naturally," she went on, sighing in a world-weary voice, "when I grow tired of him I shall also have many gallants."

"I wonder you want to marry him," Marin said in great amusement. She had never encountered such a precocious child before.

"Simply because he is very rich and I shall be able to have all the jewels and clothes I desire. It must be very tedious being poor. Uncle Charles gambles so his pockets are always to let and he has to beg the blunt from Mama. I am determined that shall never happen to *me*."

She seated herself on the bed and bounced up and down on it several times whilst Marin watched her in amazement.

"You will have your own portion surely."

"Yes, indeed, but on my marriage that will become the property of my husband and I will derive no benefit. However, Sir Hugo is said to be one of the richest men in England and I do love beautiful jewels. Don't you?"

Marin smiled. "I have never possessed any."

Caroline looked at her askance. "How dreadful! Are your parents dreadfully poor?"

"They are both dead now but we were not so poor. Where I lived, in Norfolk, there was little call to wear jewels."

"Do you have any other relatives?" the girl asked eagerly. "I am an only child."

"I have a sister who is married."

"Is she also here in London?"

Marin smiled faintly at the thought of what her sister would say if she could see her. At the reminder of what she had left behind she experienced a flicker of guilt and determined to send a note to Charity at the earliest possible moment assuring her she was safe and well.

"Marin...?"

She returned her attention to the girl, answering, "My sister lives quietly in the country, Caroline."

"How dull for her! Is there no one else?"

"Well...I did have a brother but he ran away from home about fifteen years ago and we have not heard of him since. It is a great sadness to me."

The girl clasped her hands together. "How romantic. Would it not be wonderful if you could find him again?"

"Indeed it would." Marin looked sad. "But I fear there is little chance of that."

There was a short silence between them and then, precocious as ever, Caroline said, "Why have you come to stay with us now?"

Once again Marin was uncertain and then answered as truthfully as she could,

"My parents are dead and I have nowhere else to go."

"I am persuaded you have been brought to London to find a husband."

"Oh no, that is not so!"

"Why else have you come?"

"Lady Silverwood invited me to stay here for a while."

Caroline smiled. "It is as I said; you will find a husband. You are of the correct age to be married. There is nothing else for a woman to do save marry and have a brood of children."

Marin looked bewildered. "I had not thought of such a thing."

"You do wish to be married, do you not?"

"Why yes, but I hadn't considered it yet."

The girl looked pleased. "It will be so diverting to see how matters develop. You have no notion how boring life is for me at the moment. I am not a child and yet I am still confined to the schoolroom under the discipline of a governess who happens to be a prosy old bore."

"Caroline, I am not here to seek a husband."

The girl began to look impatient. "Non-sense; whether you wish it or not you will find young bucks paying court to you. You are quite fetching, you know."

Marin blushed but her mind was in a whirl. Too much had happened so suddenly for anything to make a deal of sense and although she regarded herself as the most fortunate creature in the world, deep down inside there was a hard knot of unease.

"Shall you marry for love or fortune, Marin?"

The older girl smiled. "When I do wed I hope it will be for love."

"Mama always says if one has fortune, it is possible to find love."

Marin looked down at her hand in dismay. This kind of Society was wholly alien to what she had always been brought up to believe in, and once more a feeling of disquiet assailed her.

"You need have no fear," Caroline assured her and Marin looked at her sharply. "I heard Uncle Charles saying you would have no trouble in finding a husband."

Marin was once more taken aback, but no longer was she outraged at this girl's impudence in eavesdropping. "Indeed? And to whom did he confide this?"

Caroline grinned. "Sir Hugo as they were about to leave. I was hiding on the upper landing and they did not see me but I could hear all that they said perfectly well."

Marin shifted uncomfortably. "Did... did Sir Hugo agree with Lord Devaney?"

"One cannot expect him to. His taste in females is exquisite, you see. His fancy, I am well aware, at the moment lies with an actress from the Drury Lane Theatre whose beauty is quite breathtaking. He just laughed at Uncle Charles and said there was no possibility."

Marin's lips clamped into a thin line and her shoulders straightened as she stared ferociously into the fire. Sir Hugo during their short acquaintance had caused her many contradictory emotions but just at that moment Marin hated him thoroughly and mused it would be very satisfying to prove him wrong. In any event she had every intention of trying to do so.

Seven

"What do you think of my protégée now, Hugo?"

Lady Silverwood put one hand on his arm and looked up at him as he gazed across the room to where Marin was seated. She was surrounded by admirers who were also guests at the rout to which they had all been invited.

Sir Hugo had, in fact, been observing her for some time and it amazed him how well and quickly she had been accepted into fashionable circles, although having the patronage of so illustrious a lady as Elspeth Silverwood ensured that this would be so. It was the girl who surprised him more; she behaved as though she had been born and bred into the *haute ton*. The young men of the *beau monde* appeared to find her entrancing, which came as a surprise to him.

Lady Silverwood had, true to her word, provided the girl with suitable apparel which made a distinct improvement. On that particular evening she was wearing a gown of cornflower blue velvet embroidered with gold braid and wore feathers in her hair dyed to match the colour of the gown—and her eyes.

"I am impressed," he admitted, transferring his attention to Lady Silverwood.

"You must now be willing to concede that Charles has a good chance of winning his wager."

Sir Hugo allowed his quizzing glass to fall. "Alas, I fear that he might, although I suspect some cheating is involved and I am tempted to withdraw because of it."

Lady Silverwood drew back slightly. "How so, Hugo? The terms were perfectly simple as far as I recall."

"From what I have observed some considerable effort is being put into the venture by you. Her clothes look to be new and expensive to me, not made-over cast-offs which I believed you were intending to provide."

"But that is not cheating," she answered playfully. "It is merely an investment and you must own I am not so foolhardy in matters of money as my brother. Oh no, dearest Hugo, you do not escape so easily.

Admit it, though; this wager is hugely diverting."

"I will defer judgement upon that until the outcome is known."

Marin rose to her feet at that moment and was led towards the dance floor by one of the blades who had been paying court to her. Sir Hugo and Lady Silverwood watched them go and then Lady Silverwood said, "We are doing her a kindness. She will choose her own partner naturally, and if we derive some amusement and profit in the process it will only be our just reward for helping her achieve the kind of life she craves."

"I am not at all certain she knows what she wants. After all, my dear, there are many shades of Society between the harsh one she has come from and the one into which we have thrust her."

"Observe her carefully, Hugo. She is enjoying herself hugely, far more than we do, in fact. It is all novel to her. In fact I envy her enthusiasm for all we do; it has become tedious to me, I own."

"Not too tedious, I trust, as I do believe we are engaged to stand up together for this dance."

She gave him a smile of pure pleasure and

allowed him to lead her on to the floor where sets were being made up.

When the dance ended with a flourish Marin laughed with delight at her partner, a young army lieutenant by the name of Vernon Ripley whom she found to be a diverting companion. He was just about to take her back to her seat when a figure loomed before them. Marin looked up in alarm to see Sir Hugo standing in their way.

He bowed stiffly. "I believe I am engaged to stand up for the next dance with you, Miss Ambrose."

Marin had been aware of his presence for some time and was vexed to discover she considered him to be the most imposing man present despite her enjoyment of the company of so many others. He was so tall that his excellently cut evening attire looked magnificent on such broad shoulders, but beneath those despised opinions she still harboured resentment towards him for his tactless remarks.

He flustered her as no other man had succeeded in doing. She had found she could respond to anyone else with the correct degree of demure charm they declared both novel and delightful.

Before she had any chance to reply Lieutenant Ripley left them together but not before engaging her to go in to supper with him, something for which she was grateful. She experienced no feelings of uncertainty with Lieutenant Ripley.

"An excellent young man," Sir Hugo observed as he went into the crowd which was milling around the dance floor.

Marin could not prevent the colour creeping up her cheeks as she answered breathlessly, "Indeed. I find him vastly amusing."

He looked at her askance, hearing her utter so arch a comment. "He is, it would appear, devoted to you, Miss Ambrose."

She smiled behind her fan. "Does it surprise you that anyone should be, Sir Hugo?"

Urbane as ever he replied, "I am only surprised there are not a score more of them."

"There are. At least, not a score, more like half a score, but sufficient to keep me diverted, you must know. Lieutenant Ripley is the younger son of the Earl of Donniston."

Sir Hugo smiled. "I know the family well." He guided her towards the dance floor where sets were being made up for a country dance. "I note that you dance very gracefully."

The hated colour crept up her cheeks once more. "My family would be horrified to know how well I have taken to this life. I love dancing in particular."

He looked amused and she fixed her attention on the diamond pin he wore in his neckcloth, above a snowy ruffle of lace.

"It would appear the fact causes you some anxiety."

"I fear I was too long in my previous mode of living to dismiss it so easily."

"So you are still the little puritan at heart."

Marin bridled at his gentle mockery. "I am what I am," she retorted enigmatically, and at this he laughed.

"Indeed you are, and no one is more delighted to note it than I."

She averted her face. She was beginning to realise there was no manner in which she could best him and understood the better now his reputation.

After a moment's pause she said in a more subdued voice, "I hope you and Lord Devaney do not mind that I have written a short note to my sister informing her that I am safe and well."

One eyebrow rose a fraction. "Why should we mind? It was your wish to leave home, not ours. It was thoughtful of you to consider her..."

"Oh, I am well aware she will merely tear up the note and pretend she has never received it, but she will be concerned for me even though she will consider me an ingrate and a sinner."

"Do you not fear she will come in pursuit of you?"

"I made no mention of my present address, but neither she nor my brother-in-law will pursue me. As in the case of my brother, I will now be totally cast off and my name forbidden to be mentioned by any member of the family."

The dance commenced and conversation was precluded for a while, much to Marin's relief. She could dance far better than she was able to converse with this enigma of a man. All the while she was aware that as partners they generated a deal of interest from the others present. It seemed that Sir Hugo was a man about whom everyone was eager to talk. Suddenly she held her head higher, for she realised she had been honoured indeed.

"Has life in Lady Silverwood's circle lived up to your expectations?" he asked when they came together again.

"I had no expectations at all, Sir Hugo, but I have never enjoyed myself so much." She chuckled then. "Mayhap it is truer to say I have never enjoyed myself before." Suddenly she grew sober again. "So much has been given me I am bewildered by it so I feel a little guilty for wishing I could also trace my brother."

Sir Hugo studied her carefully for a moment or two. "You were, I believe, resigned to consider him dead."

"I fear that must be true, but I would rest happier if I knew for certain. But," she added philosophically, "one cannot have *everything*."

"Why not?" he asked, arching his eyebrows once more.

She had no opportunity to answer if indeed she was able, for they were obliged to part once again. When they came together once more she said, "Lady Silverwood is planning to hold a masquerade at Silverwood House as the last big function of the Season. It sounds to be a most exciting occurrence. We shall all be obliged to wear special costumes!"

He gazed at her for a long moment, quite moved by the excitement generated by so mundane an occasion as a masquerade.

"Shall *you* be present, Sir Hugo?"

"I would not miss it for anything. Have you decided on what costume you will wear?"

Marin dimpled. "I cannot say. Lady Silverwood has planned something for me but I am sworn to secrecy."

"Then I shall not press you, but you may rest easy that if Lady Silverwood has a hand in the matter you will be clad in a spectacular costume."

"Do you know yet what costume you will be wearing, Sir Hugo?"

"I have not given the matter much thought as yet."

"I ask only because we will all be masked until midnight—so it is like we shall not know each other."

His lips curved into the semblance of a smile as he replied in a soft voice, "Do you think not, Miss Ambrose?"

For a while she had forgotten her awkwardness in his company but suddenly she was discomforted once more and lapsed into an embarrassed silence. She had been enjoying herself hugely, for he was an excellent partner, but when the dance came to an end she was relieved. More than ever conscious of him at her side she walked slowly back to where she had previously been sitting.

As they approached the sofa around which some of her new acquaintances were grouped Marin stopped and turned to him once more. Her eyes once again were level with the diamond pin which winked and sparkled beneath the light of hundreds of candles.

"Sir Hugo, one matter has been troubling me greatly..."

He put his head slightly to one side whilst regarding her silently and she went on in a more muted tone, "Do you still regard me guilty of the crime Squire Chawton accused me of?"

He looked surprised, as well he might. "Naturally not. Having seen young Joseph Chawton, I have no doubt about the cravenness of his nature. I would not tolerate you to be taken into Lady Silverwood's house if I believed such a thing true of you."

She smiled faintly. "You are fond, are you not, of Lady Silverwood?"

"My feelings for Lady Silverwood were not the subject of your question, Miss Ambrose. I cannot imagine why you ask it of me now."

"Simply because I have the feeling you still do not entirely trust me."

The sleepy look in his eyes vanished and a steely look came into them. "What makes you think so?"

Lowering her gaze she murmured, feeling foolish now. "It is merely a feeling I have. Perhaps I am being ungenerous but it does grieve me."

She raised her eyes once more to find him staring at her stonily. "Let it grieve you no longer. I may regard you as foolhardy in leaving your home for a world you could not possibly know, but I can certainly understand your reasons for doing so. What really grieves you, Miss Ambrose?" he asked in a soft yet resolute voice. "Perchance it is the fact that you cannot number me amongst that half score adoring admirers?"

She gasped at so unexpected an accusation and stepped back a pace. Her eyes grew darker and were filled with pain. "You are mistaken, Sir Hugo."

He smiled crookedly. "You seem to be favoured by so many people, Miss Ambrose, is it so necessary for you to have my approval too?"

Marin was still trying to find an answer when her next partner came to claim her. Sir Hugo made a stiff bow to them both before turning abruptly on his heel and striding away. Marin bit her lip as she watched him go. Just when he seemed to warm to her he had grown hostile again and it gave her no satisfaction to know that it was entirely her own fault on this occasion. Her eyes involuntarily filled with tears, for she could not understand why his good will was so important to her.

"Miss Ambrose . . . ?"

Her partner was looking at her curiously and after a moment or two she forced a smile to her face and allowed him to lead her into the set. As she took her place she looked around for sight of Sir Hugo, but she could not see him anywhere in the room and her spirits sank to an even lower level. Drat the man, she thought bitterly; he was quite correct in his assumption. Of all the men who had been enslaved by her charm, Sir Hugo was the only one she wished to entrance, be it only for the pleasure of breaking his heart....

Eight

Marin stood at the drawing window gazing down into Park Lane, where a succession of elegant carriages were moving to and from the Park.

"Lieutenant Ripley seems to be quite entranced by you," Viscount Devaney told her.

Marin's cheeks grew pink, something she abhorred but others found delightful in her. She turned to face the room where Lady Silverwood reclined on a day bed by the fire being fed marchpane by her Negro pageboy.

"Mr Ethelston too," she pointed out. "Last night at Vauxhall he was scarce able to take his eyes off you all evening. He is well-connected on his mother's side."

Marin laced her fingers together. "Lord Devaney, there is something I would ask of you. Advice..."

"Of course, my dear, ask of me anything you wish."

Lady Silverwood's eyes narrowed

thoughtfully as she considered Marin. "That shade of blue of your gown is not right for you. When you take it off do not wear it again."

"As you wish, Lady Silverwood."

"Now dear, what was it you wanted Lord Devaney to give you advice about?"

"As you say these gentlemen pay me court and I am very flattered by it..."

He smiled. "You have no need to be. Your looks are quite entrancing and your manner is pleasing to all those with a modicum of sensibility."

"I realise that a great deal of flirtation is practised by everyone but what if one of them is in earnest? What if," she went on in some difficulty, "one of them offers for me?"

Lord Devaney and his sister exchanged significant looks before he asked in a deceptively mild way, "Have you any reason to believe that one of them is about to?"

Marin shook her head. "No, but I did wonder what I should do in the event."

Lord Devaney chuckled heartily. "Accept with alacrity, my dear."

"In all fairness, Charles," his sister said, nibbling at the sweetmeat thoughtfully, "it is not likely of Lieutenant Ripley, for whatever his feelings for *you*, Marin, he must needs seek a wealthy bride."

"He is the son of an earl," Marin pointed out.

Lady Silverwood smiled at her naivete. "A younger son. Oh, I do not doubt he has his allowance and of course his army pay, but it will not be great. Naturally, though, if he is so taken by you it will make no odds that you have no portion. Such alliances have taken place before." She hesitated before asking, "What are your feelings for him, my dear?"

Marin lowered her eyes. "He is an exceedingly pleasant companion."

She did not notice the look of satisfaction which passed between the other two before Lady Silverwood asked, "If he does come up to scratch, would you accept?"

Strangely enough this was one point she had not yet considered and was for the moment at a loss for an answer. But then she recalled what Sir Hugo had said of her marriage prospects in Caroline's hearing and she stiffened with resolution.

"Yes, I believe I would be inclined to do so, but," she added hastily, "I am by no means certain."

Lady Silverwood sank back onto her

daybed looking more than a little satisfied. "Of course there are others and you will have the opportunity to choose, I am certain, so do not have intractible thoughts on the subject just yet. There is time."

Marin let out a sigh of relief. "Yes, I shall think on it carefully when the time comes."

Lord Devaney took his leave of them and when he had gone his sister said, "Marin dear, I think it time to issue invitations for the masquerade. Would you be so good as to write them for me? I note your hand is neat."

"I should be glad to be of service to you, Lady Silverwood," Marin answered truthfully.

"Good. You will find the guest list in my escritoire in the library, and there is also a supply of invitations too. You may do it now, for Lord Thornway is due to call at any time and I would like to receive him in private."

Marin hurried towards the door. "Of course. I shall go immediately and see you at dinner."

"And do not forget we are going to the Opera tonight. It will be a gala event and I'm persuaded you will enjoy the experience."

Marin grinned. "I could not forget anything, Lady Silverwood. It is all so new and exciting to me."

When she had closed the door behind her Lady Silverwood allowed herself a chuckle before applying herself to the marchpane once more.

An hour later Marin came out of the library with the pile of invitations in her hand. Her head ached slightly from the effort of completing the task but she was glad to have it done. A constant rapping of her knuckles in childhood had ensured the perfection of her hand.

One of Lady Silverwood's footmen was coming towards her as she walked down the corridor, and still unaccustomed to ordering servants to do her bidding, she asked rather apologetically, "Could you see that these are delivered, please?"

The footman bowed and held out a silver salver. "Certainly, ma'am. It shall be done immediately." There was an envelope on the salver and he went on, "This message has just arrived for you, ma'am. The man who delivered it stressed that it was urgent."

Marin took it rather gingerly from the tray. "For me?" she murmured.

She stared at it for some moments whilst the footman bore away the invitations. It was her own name written upon it and when she turned it over the seal was that of an eagle surrounded by a sprig of myrtle. The missive had an important air about it but messages she received from admirers were invariably written on calling cards. After hesitating fractionally she tore it open, her eyes widening when she discovered just who had written it.

The message was characteristically terse. "WILL CALL FOR YOU AT 3 O'CLOCK. BE PREPARED FOR A RIDE IN MY CARRIAGE. TRULY YOURS, HUGO LYTTON BT."

Marin had little time to feel bewildered, for at that moment the long case clock in the hall struck a quarter to three and knowing how angry he was likely to be if she had the temerity to be late she flew up the stairs, almost cannoning into Caroline on the landing.

"Just the person I was seeking," the girl declared. "Will you play chess with me this afternoon? Miss Falkingham has one of her headaches and has gone to lie down on her bed."

"Oh, I am sorry, Caroline. I wish I could oblige for my game is improving, but I cannot. I must go out."

The girl's glance inevitably strayed to the letter which was still clutched in Marin's hand and her eyes began to gleam. "Is that a *billet doux*? Do you have a secret assignation this afternoon? Oh, do tell me!"

Marin stiffened with indignation. "It is nothing of the kind, you may be sure. Sir Hugo is to take me out in his carriage although I cannot conceive why."

Caroline's eyes grew round. "In his carriage! That's a very interesting development."

"Why?" Marin asked.

"If a gentleman takes a lady riding alone in his carriage in the Park everyone will expect an announcement of the betrothal before long."

Marin smiled bitterly. "Well, I think you can be sure Sir Hugo will not be taking me into the Park."

"I cannot conceive why you are so certain. After all you do have several suitors so mayhap Sir Hugo wishes to become one of them."

She began to giggle behind her hand and

Marin laughed too. "That is impossible. I would not wish to spoil *your* chances for the future."

Caroline grinned back at her. "It is not my chances which concern me any longer. I am beginning to believe you are right and he is too old, but you will invite Mama's wrath if you catch his fancy."

Marin, aware of the passing of time, began to back away from her. "Sir Hugo and I, if the truth be known, do not get on very well. In fact, the last time we met we parted in a rather hostile way. That is why this invitation is such a surprise."

"It might be his way of apologising."

"Not Sir Hugo. He would never apologise!"

"He is as proud as Lucifer, Mama says, and he can be very difficult," Caroline agreed, running alongside her, "but agreeable men can become so boring after a while."

Marin paused to stare at her. That remark seemed rather mature for one of such tender years, but then, belatedly, she realised she could not compare this girl with any she had known before.

"Be a dear, Caroline, and help me change my gown. I have no time to call a maid and cannot possibly manage myself in so short a time."

Caroline began to unhook Marin's gown. "I knew having you here would be diverting!" she said gleefully. "I keep hoping two of your suitors will fight a duel!"

Marin chuckled as she stepped out of the skirts. "Vile creature! I would die of mortification and I would not for anything have blood spilled on my account."

"You are indeed a very strange person, Marin," Caroline answered, shaking her head sagely.

It was just before the clock struck three that Marin came hurrying down the stairs, pulling on her gloves as she did so. She had changed into a brown silk gown with matching pelisse and bonnet trimmed with feathers which sat at a jaunty angle atop the confusion of golden curls Lady Silverwood's hairdresser had created for her. The acceptance of all Lady Silverwood had bestowed upon her continued to cause Marin some anguish, for the gowns set out for her use seemed far too good and fashionable to be hand-me-downs, but Lady Silverwood insisted that they were. If Marin did not make use of them they would only be packed away in camphor.

As she glanced out of the landing window on her way downstairs she saw a smart high-perch phaeton pull into the courtyard. It was a magnificent vehicle, painted a bright yellow with the Lytton coat of arms emblazoned on the sides. A team of matched grey mares pulled it and the moment they had come to a halt Sir Hugo jumped down and handed the ribbons to his groom.

She watched him stride up to the house, his caped greatcoat flapping about him. Her heart was beating unaccountably fast but by the time he was admitted to the house she was walking down the stairs to meet him and appeared composed.

He stood in the hall, looking up at her, and even though the gown had once belonged to Lady Silverwood Marin knew that it became her colouring better and he would have no cause to feel ashamed of her.

"You are very prompt," he greeted her.

She concentrated her attention on his highly polished hessians from which golden tassels swung. "You would not countenance any other behaviour, Sir Hugo, even though I was sorely pressed to be ready on time."

He smiled as she preceded him out of the house. "You will find the effort worthwhile," he promised and she gave him a curious look.

"Oh yes, no doubt I shall, for I am given to understand this is a great honour."

They paused by the carriage and Marin would have loved to have patted the horses but they looked so disciplined and well-groomed she dare not.

"Let us cry pax, Miss Ambrose," he suggested and when she looked at him sharply an amused light shone from his dark eyes.

"Sir Hugo, I was not aware we were engaged in a state of war."

"Are we not?"

She turned her head away. "That would be totally alien to one brought up as I."

"So is your life in London, but I am persuaded you are enjoying it heartily."

He handed her up into the carriage and she was aware of the feel of his hand as with no one else. When he had climbed up beside her the groom handed him the ribbons and they set off. Just as the phaeton turned into Park Lane a curricle driven by one of her suitors turned in and the driver stared at them in astonishment as they went past, Marin inclining her head in acknowledgement.

"I fear that Mr Ethelson is not pleased to have missed you," Sir Hugo remarked as he flicked his whip over the back of his team.

"I was not expecting him to call so he has no cause to feel displeased."

"You are quite hard-hearted, Miss Ambrose."

Ignoring the irony in his voice she asked, "Would it be presumptuous of me to enquire where we are going?"

"For a drive," he answered.

"To the Park?" she could not help but ask.

"No." He glanced at her with a renewal of interest then. "Would you prefer that we did?"

Mindful of what Caroline had told her she answered, "No!" and he looked amused once more. "I wonder that you are troubling to spend time with me at all after the manner in which we last parted."

They were, as she expected, receiving a good share of attention as the carriage bowled towards Tyburn and the Oxford Road.

"I am often a sorehead, Miss Ambrose, and I am certain you know it. Please make allowances. I take my pleasures seriously."

"Pleasures, Sir Hugo?"

"The fact is, I enjoy crossing words with you."

"That is a strange sort of sport, even for you, Sir Hugo."

He continued to look amused. "If you will but admit it, you must also grow weary of the fatuous compliments showered on you from every quarter."

Her lips curved into a smile. "No female ever born would have enough of that."

"You disappoint me."

Still smiling she answered, "Ah yes, I know."

"Doesn't polite conversation become wearying occasionally?"

"I can assure you it does not. It is at the basis of all civilised society."

"But there is the barbarian in all of us."

Despite the warmth of the day she shivered and gave her attention to the much more comfortable prospect of the shops along the Oxford Road which never failed to attract her. The myriad selection of luxury goods they offered made them appear a treasure trove to her and she enjoyed nothing better than to visit them with Lady Silverwood just for the joy of handling the beauteous merchandise.

Soon they were approaching an area with which Marin was not yet familiar and she was just viewing it with interest when Sir Hugo said, "You really haven't forgiven me for suspecting you of theft, have you, Miss Ambrose?" Her head snapped back to regard him coldly and he went on, "To someone of your strict upbringing there could hardly be a worse accusation, only perhaps that of immoral behaviour, but you must appreciate that the situation appeared most suspicious at the time."

Marin continued to stare at his haughty profile for a few moments longer before turning away once more. "I assure you, I have dismissed the matter from my mind."

It was almost true, for the fact he regarded her as unlikely to be considered for a wife by any of his exalted acquaintances rankled far more.

Sir Hugo drove the high-perch phaeton into a pleasant square surrounded by houses on every side. When the phaeton came to a halt outside one of them she looked at him quizzically but he said nothing; he merely climbed down and offered his hand. She gazed down into his inscrutable face, wishing for once to know what his thoughts and feelings might be. In others it was easy to judge but with him impossible, and yet she felt someone must know the real Hugo Lytton. Lady Silverwood perhaps.

Sir Hugo quirked one eyebrow. "Miss Ambrose?"

"Where are we?" she asked, feigning a carefree attitude.

"Bloomsbury Square."

"And pray tell me why we are here?"

"To pay a visit, of course." She continued to hesitate and he said in some amusement, "There is no ogre behind that door. No Squire Chawton ready to spring at you."

His ridicule had the desired effect and she allowed him to help her down. She followed him up the narrow path whereupon he rattled at the highly-polished knocker. The door was opened some moments later by a manservant and although the house they were shown into was nowhere near as large or impressive as the ones she had become used to of late it was certainly handsome. Whoever they had come to visit must be a person of means.

The manservant led the way to an upstairs drawing room after having divested Sir Hugo of his coat, hat and gloves. Marin felt rather apprehensive, for she could not imagine why she had been brought here. Instinctively she trusted Sir Hugo but all the while she was not certain she was right to do so.

When they were ushered into the drawing room, which overlooked the square, there was only one other man present. He was an extremely handsome man, being almost as tall as Sir Hugo and broad of shoulder. He was well-dressed but certainly not foppish and his fair hair was caught back in a ribbon, the style which most young men favoured even though older men still clung to the habit of wearing their wigs.

When they entered he took a few steps forward limping slightly and Sir Hugo said, drawing her forward, "Captain Ambrose, allow me to present your sister to you."

So unexpected was this encounter for a moment Marin could only stare at the other man who was equally transfixed.

"Prudence?" he said hopefully after a moment. "My little Prudence, is it really you?"

"Matthew," she sighed at last, her face becoming alight with wonder.

And then, hesitating no longer, she rushed into his arms.

"You were so little when I last saw you, no more than a babe."

"I always dreamed of finding you one day but never dared to hope that I would."

Sir Hugo moved back towards the door. "You will have a great deal to talk about so I shall return later."

"Thank you, Sir Hugo," Marin said gratefully and then immediately gave her attention to her brother once more.

"How fine you look," he told her. "Oh, 'tis wonderful to see you, my dear. Come along and sit with me and tell me all about yourself."

"Oh, there is little enough to tell, but how did Sir Hugo find you, and so quickly too?"

"I believe it was remarkably easy. We are both members of Watier's."

She reached out to touch his hand, still not daring to believe he was truly her brother. "We shall always be in his debt, Matthew."

"Indeed."

He could not take his eyes off her and she said shyly, "I still cannot believe I am not dreaming this."

"Nor I." At last he roused himself to say, "I understand Papa is dead."

She nodded. "Of the apoplexy more than a year ago. It was mercifully quick."

Captain Ambrose sighed. "It was wrong of me to leave home as I did, but after Mama died I had to go. My feelings towards him became so unforgiving. You see, I always regarded him to blame for her demise. You could not know, but she was worn out giving birth to still-born children, all of them between Charity and you. She was frail and the life he imposed upon her was too harsh. Neither was she as committed to it as he."

"I never knew," she murmured, "but I believe I suspected it was so."

"How is Charity?"

Marin smiled. "She is well. She has married a very worthy fellow, but I will not say she is happy, for such an emotion would be alien to her."

He laughed. "How right you are. I suppose it is just that one of Papa's children is a virtuous person."

"I believe that we can be considered virtuous, Matthew, but we are not *saintly.*"

"May I send for some wine, or a dish of tea?"

"No! I am far too excited to partake of one

134

drop, and I do not wish to waste a moment of my time with you. Tell me what you did when you left home."

"I joined the army and had the good luck to become a captain in due course."

"You must have been an exceedingly good soldier to rise through the ranks."

He laughed deprecatingly. "Foolhardy is mayhap more like the truth."

"Do go on, Matthew. I am in a fever to know all about you."

"I went to fight in America when the war first broke out but an injury to my leg soon resulted in a discharge. After I had recovered I decided to try my luck in the Indies where there are opportunities to make a fortune. Those islands are wonderful places and I was again fortunate there. When I finally returned to England it was as a fairly wealthy man." He laughed. "I became everything that Papa considered sinful. As a gentleman of substance I indulged in every vice I knew our father would abhor, but I am over that now and lead a much quieter life.

"And now tell me all about yourself. I believe you call yourself by another name now."

"Marin is not so puritanical as Prudence, which you must own does not suit me at all."

They both laughed and he said, "Even as a mere babe I suspected you and I were alike in many ways. I thought of you from time to time and wondered how you fared in that awful place. If I had known you were so unhappy I would have come for you."

"It is of no matter now, Matthew. We have found each other at last and we shall not be parted again."

He clasped her hand in his. "We shall see each other often that is certain. How I wish I had a wife and could offer you a home with me."

Her countenance took on a look of dismay. "It is of no matter. Because you are not wed I am able to come here and keep house for you. Charity taught me to be a good housekeeper."

"I do not doubt it," he said gently, "but even so it will not do. You must seek your own home now you are of a marriageable age. Sir Hugo tells me you have several suitors of quality."

"I really care nothing for any of them if the truth is known."

He leaned forward. "Listen to me, Marin.

This is an opportunity you cannot afford to miss. Lady Silverwood is known to me and she will provide a passage for you into the correct circles which is most important. I cannot do so much for you."

"They have all been so kind to me, Matthew, but sometimes I do wonder why."

"Sir Hugo confided to me the circumstances of your meeting and I shudder when I think of the dangers you faced alone and unprotected. I dare not think of what would have become of you if he and Lord Devaney had not taken pity on you. Marin," he went on uncertainly, "I am not a poor men, but I cannot do for you what Lady Silverwood is able. What I am able to do is repay Lord Devaney for any expense incurred on your behalf. I have also arranged for a portion of money to be set aside for your marriage settlement and an allowance for your everyday expenses. Your future is now assured. A marriage should be easy to arrange."

"Oh Matthew, that is not necessary. By all means settle your account with Lord Devaney and Lady Silverwood, but whoever wishes to marry me will do so regardless of my prospects."

He smiled faintly. "Alas, that is not true.

Most men require some kind of settlement from their betrothed."

"Any men of that calibre need not trouble to pay court to me," she answered heatedly.

He smiled again. "You know nothing of the fashionable world, my dear. Your head is still full of dreams. There are few enough men able to afford a wife with no portion, and those who are aspire to high rank.

"Allow me to do this for you, Marin. It will give me much pleasure."

She nodded before saying, "I will not disown my connection with you, Matthew."

"That will not be necessary. I promise we will meet often. In fact, Sir Hugo has been gracious enough to invite me to dinner with you all on Friday next."

Marin's eyes gleamed. "I had no notion he was so good."

"Nor I. He and I are members of Watier's and we have mutual friends, but our paths have not crossed before. I must confess, Marin, up until now I had no real liking for the fellow. He's a true Corinthian and I admire his style but..." He looked at her keenly then. "I scarce know how to say this, but he has a certain reputation as a rake... Marin, I trust he has not..."

Her cheeks grew rosy and she averted her

eyes. "Oh no, Matthew. I assure you there is nothing of that sort." She toyed with the braiding on her skirt. "In fact I am persuaded Sir Hugo regards me as a poor specimen of a female. As I have said I cannot conceive why he and Lord Devaney have taken me up in this way."

Captain Ambrose shrugged. "Nor I. I can only surmise that there is in them a fund of goodness we know nothing about."

Marin looked happier then. "I am persuaded that must be the answer. We have so many years to catch up on, Matthew."

"Sir Hugo will be returning shortly to take you back to Silverwood House, but I shall see you on Friday."

"There is to be a masquerade at Silverwood House soon; I will prevail upon Lady Silverwood to issue an invitation to you."

"I shall not make any attempt to dissuade you from such a course, for I would be delighted to renew my acquaintance with her."

He smiled to himself at the thought and then the manservant interrupted to announce the return of Sir Hugo Lytton.

Nine

The dining room of Sir Hugo Lytton's London home was handsomely appointed. Marble pillars supported a vast ceiling painted with scenes of nymphs and cupids gathering fruits. It was all Marin could do to restrain herself from craning her neck to look at them all the time. Instead she considered the paintings by Gainsborough and Reynolds adorning the walls and the valuable statues which stood in alcoves at intervals between them.

A long mahogany table monopolised the room which was lit by sparkling crystal chandeliers ablaze with hundreds of candles and also by silver-gilt candelabra set at intervals along the table. A dazzling selection of dessert dishes were spread along the table, to be eaten with gold spoons and forks. A silver-gilt epergne dominated the table and was overflowing with out-of-season fruit and tropical specialities which Marin had never seen before.

She ate her dinner almost in silence, happy to be in the company of her brother once again. He was, she discovered, totally at ease in the company of Sir Hugo and his guests. For a great deal of the time he kept them entertained by recounting his exploits in the early days of the American War and his subsequent adventures in the Indies.

"The war still goes badly," ventured one lady who had been regarding Captain Ambrose with admiration throughout the evening. "Do you think we shall lose the colonies after all?"

"I fear that may be the outcome of the sorry business," he replied.

"You have led an enviably full life, Captain Ambrose," Lady Silverwood remarked, eyeing him though her crystal wineglass.

"Perhaps I felt the necessity to make up for my first seventeen years which were totally uneventful save for the beatings my father felt duty-bound to give me from time to time."

He glanced at Marin who smiled at him sympathetically. "It grieves me," he went on, "after so many trials and tribulations to return to England and find so much upheaval here at home."

"It is only a small faction, Captain Ambrose," Sir Hugo pointed out, having been content up until then, like Marin, to be silent for most of the time.

"When someone as insane as Lord George Gordon is intent upon causing mischief," Lady Silverwood murmured, "one can never be certain where it will end."

"It is horrifying," Marin ventured timidly.

Lord Devaney looked at her indulgently. He was always unfailingly kind to her, unlike Sir Hugo, and yet it had been he who had found Matthew for her.

"It need not concern you," he told her. "Lord George Gordon will find no sympathy for his extreme views and the protest will die a natural death."

The matter was then discussed in more detail and Marin's eyes came to rest on Sir Hugo. With a start she discovered he had been gazing at her and when their eyes met his lips curved into a smile which caused her to look away quickly. For once, though, she was certain she had seen real warmth in his eyes and the realisation pleased her.

"The answer is for the military to act decisively to stamp out any insurrection," Captain Ambrose stated and Marin was astonished to see that Lady Silverwood was attending him with great interest, her eyes sparkling and her lips curved into a smile of indulgence.

"One can only wish," she said with a sigh, "that a man of your calibre was in charge of those who protect us, but I fear we are not so fortunate."

Despite herself Marin found her attention wandering to Sir Hugo once more. How handsome he is, she thought, and not for the first time. The whiteness of the lace at his throat contrasted starkly against the darkness of his features which were now in profile. The breeding of centuries was stamped on his bearing which in any situation would display enormous pride.

Her gaze strayed to each of the other men present in turn and she was shocked to discover she could not look upon them in so favourable a light as Sir Hugo. When she returned her attention to him again he was speaking to Lady Silverwood in soft tones and the woman laughed gaily at what had been said.

Marin was surprised and dismayed to find she resented that little intimacy between them, even though she was well aware of their long-standing relationship.

She had not dwelt upon it since her arrival in London but now she began to speculate upon that relationship which was starting to intrigue her. Suddenly the thought of them being in love, perhaps about to wed, caused anguish to twist inside her like a sharp-bladed knife.

At that moment Sir Hugo became aware of her hard scrutiny and he looked at her quizzically. "Miss Ambrose, you do not appear to be eating. Do you not find the junket to your taste?"

Marin smiled faintly. "It is excellent, Sir Hugo, as was the rest of the meal, only I believe I have eaten too much."

"Nonsense, you eat like a bird," Lady Silverwood retorted.

Sir Hugo rose from his chair. "Perhaps the ladies would like to withdraw now," he suggested and Marin was the first of them to rise, unaccountably glad to leave the men to their port.

"At least with so many of us present you will not drink yourselves senseless," Lady Silverwood remarked as she rose to her feet, much to the amusement of the others.

"The company on this evening is far too delightful for us to linger too long," Sir Hugo answered.

"I certainly agree," Lord Devaney said, "but nevertheless, Hugo, your port is too good to hurry."

When Marin reached the door she paused to allow the other ladies to catch up with her, for she was alone in not knowing where the drawing room was situated. As she turned to glance back Sir Hugo's eyes were upon her and once again she quickly looked away.

She lagged behind the other ladies as they walked through a gallery where many fine portraits were hung. They all attracted her interest, for they seemed without exception to be of Sir Hugo's ancestors. It was plain to see his dark looks had been passed down from generation to generation.

She was gazing at one of them when Lady Silverwood came up behind her, which caused Marin to start guiltily although she was committing no wrong, save a newfound interest in this enigmatic man. "Hugo really has surpassed himself in finding your brother," Lady Silverwood remarked as she idly twirled her fan.

"I had no idea what he was about."

"Neither did I, which is more to the point," she answered drily, "but one can never be certain of the workings of his mind. I must warn you of that lest you become ... sentimental."

Marin smiled, well aware of the veiled warning in Lady Silverwood's words. "I assure you I would never be so foolish, but it *was* very kind of him."

Her eyebrows arched. "I own that it is and it is also the very first time I have ever known him to demonstrate such a quality. However, I must confess that he has done us both a kindness."

"Yes, I believe you and Matthew were once acquainted."

"Oh, it was several years ago and I am delighted to renew the acquaintance. I am most impressed by his military record."

"I am very proud to have such a brother," Marin told her warmly.

One of the other ladies beckoned Lady Silverwood over and she said in a soft voice, "Come along into the drawing room when you have finished in the gallery."

Lady Silverwood and her companion went into the drawing room which was situated at the end of the gallery whilst Marin continued to peruse the portraits one by one. Her imagination was alight with speculation and she was lost in interest until a voice at her shoulder said, "He was a favourite of Queen Elizabeth. He was in disgrace, though, from the day he married one of her ladies in waiting."

Marin turned to find Sir Hugo had come upon her unheard. The other gentlemen, including Matthew, were drifting towards the drawing room where tea would soon be served.

Sir Hugo gazed up at the portrait of his ancestor. "In fact, he spent some time in the Tower, which I think might have cooled his ardour somewhat, don't you think?"

Marin's startled look was replaced by a mischievous one. "He must have been a brave man."

"He would need to be. His wife proved to be a veritable termagent."

He moved to the next portrait. "This is his son."

"I like the look of him."

"Alas, he proved to be a blackguard. He plotted against King James and was executed for his pains."

"This gentleman looks rather splendid..."

"Ah, he was another Hugo. He fought for

King Charles during the Civil War and went into exile with his son to France."

He continued to gaze up at the portrait as Marin said, "Your ancestors seemed to thrive on intrigue."

"It was more than that in this instance. Sir Hugo—the first one of course—had a pronounced penchant for the ladies. I imagine there were a number of puritan ladies who were less than virtuous after encountering this young blade."

"Do you not feel a mite discomforted by their constant presence in your home?"

He gave her a long look which she could not meet. "Whatever my sins, Miss Ambrose, I am certain they committed graver ones. They tend to make me feel virtuous."

He took a pinch of snuff whilst Marin observed him obliquely, marvelling at the way her resentment and distrust of him had melted entirely.

"It was good of you to invite Matthew tonight," she said in a soft voice.

His own manner softened too. "He makes an entertaining guest."

As they walked along the gallery Marin said, "You have all been so good to me, but I feel better now that Matthew is providing

RACHELLE EDWARDS

for me, even though I shall never be able to repay you all for the kindness you have displayed."

"You have a strong streak of pride in you which is admirable."

"Some people would find it objectionable in a woman."

"I suspect you have suffered for it in the past."

Marin laughed wryly. "Oh, indeed, Sir Hugo. There are parts of me which tingle yet. Matthew is also, you may know, providing me with a portion..."

Sir Hugo halted in his tracks and stared at her in such a way she drew back. "I did not know," he said at last, turning away from her. He seemed dismayed, which surprised her, for she could think of no reason why he should be. "I am glad matters have ended so happily for you, Miss Ambrose."

Suddenly coquettish she said, raising her fan to hide her smile. "Nothing is ended as yet, Sir Hugo. I am yet to receive an offer of marriage, which I believe is expected of me."

"Expected, Miss Ambrose?" he asked frowningly.

"Why yes. My brother is most anxious to

see me settled." He relaxed a little and then she asked, "Do you think that I might receive an offer this Season?"

He glanced at her quickly and then away again. "With someone as fetching as you, it is entirely possible you will receive several."

Marin experienced a measure of satisfaction for she was certain she had in some way she could not fathom contrived to disconcert him. One thing she was still determined upon and that was to prove him wrong in his opinion of her.

He touched her arm and she found herself trembling beneath his touch, a phenomenon she could not understand but it had happened on other occasions. It never happened when she came into contact with other men though.

"Let us join the others, Miss Ambrose, lest they speculate on our absence."

She felt that he had withdrawn from her again, that his manner had cooled. She was at a loss to account for it but nevertheless contrived to look at him with wide-eyed innocence.

"Upon what can they possibly speculate, Sir Hugo?"

Without answering he strode over to the drawing room. As he approached a footman threw open the door and Sir Hugo waited for her to join him. Feigning a carelessness she could not possibly feel, Marin preceded him into the room where Lady Silverwood was playing the harpsichord, a skill her young protégé envied.

"Ah, Hugo," a dowager greeted him from her seat at the card table, "come try your hand at hazard."

He went to the table immediately and Marin's brother approached which gave her no opportunity to reflect on that disconcerting conversation.

"Marin, my dear, you look so lovely tonight."

Her cheeks grew pink. "I am glad I do not shame you, Matthew."

They went to sit together on a sofa to listen to Lady Silverwood's playing. "She does everything so well," Marin said, a mite resentfully.

"I confess I had forgotten how entrancing she is." He returned his attention to her. "Lord Devaney tells me several young men are paying court to you in earnest now, all of them of excellent character and prospects."

She toyed with her fan as she answered in a muted tone, "It is most flattering."

"It is now my only anxiety to see you well

settled, and this I intend to do. Is there anyone you favour, my dear?"

She shook her head and knew that this was so. She liked Lieutenant Ripley and Mr Ethelston extremely well but as for marriage...She sighed when she recalled having told Lady Silverwood she would accept one of her suitors, for in reality she was far from certain she wished to spend the remainder of her life with any one of them.

Unwillingly once more her eyes settled on Sir Hugo who was now playing hazard with Lady Gorlston and at last she knew why she was not enthusiastic about any of her suitors. It was suddenly plain to her the reason for her strange feelings in Sir Hugo's presence. It was love. Although she had never experienced such a feeling before she did not doubt that it was so. When he was absent she looked for him and yet when he was present she experienced discomfort. No other affected her in such a way.

The irony of the situation almost made her laugh out loud, for he was the one man in all the world she could not have.

Matthew startled her out of her thoughts by putting her hand over hers. "You have time in which to decide but once you do I shall feel free to pursue my own fancy."

She looked at him sharply. "Do you have someone in mind?"

He smiled and nodded. "Yes, I believe I do."

Marin followed the direction of his gaze and hers came to rest on Lady Silverwood. "Oh, Matthew," she sighed, unable to tell him that the two people they loved were interested only in each other. "You are by comparison a humble man."

"Fortunately Lady Silverwood is a lady who invariably allows her heart to rule her head. I am fully aware that the pursuit of my heart's desire will not be easy, Marin, but I have faced greater odds and won."

She looked at him curiously. "You will enjoy the challenge."

"The greater the odds the more pleasure in winning."

"So you are a gambling man too."

"Not as much as I used to be, but this will be the greatest challenge."

For a few moments she watched Sir Hugo intent upon his game of hazard with some of his guests and they appeared to be hugely enjoying themselves.

"Since my arrival in London I have witnessed a prodigious amount of gambling," Marin told him.

"'Tis a fever in the blood with men and women alike."

She looked at him with interest. "It seems that nothing is sacred. Only the other evening I overheard several gentlemen making a wager as to which of the ladies present would be called upon to sing first."

Captain Ambrose laughed. "I can well believe it. Some bizarre wagers have been recorded in the books of Watier's and Brooks. They make diverting reading, and yet the most interesting wagers are those which are never recorded."

"Sir Hugo is an inveterate gambler, I believe," she said in a careless manner which betrayed nothing of her newfound feelings.

"No more than most, but that does not mean to say he does not play deep. He can, however, withstand losses better than many, for he is extremely wealthy, few more so. I have not known him lose very often. Sir Hugo is a man who plays to win."

"It would be a sore blow to his excessive pride if he did not."

Matthew Ambrose smiled at his sister indulgently. "You have much to learn. With men like Sir Hugo Lytton pride is nothing untoward, for it is inbred for generations."

"This is not so surprising. I have seen the portraits of his illustrious ancestors in his gallery."

Her gaze returned to him once more, wishing now she was able to flirt and make clever remarks as she had observed others do so well. How she wished now she were anyone other than who she was.

"Did you receive your invitation to Lady Silverwood's masquerade?" she asked moments later.

"Personally penned by her ladyship," he answered smugly. "I have ordered my costume."

"Lady Silverwood chose mine, for I have no idea what will do, but I cannot divulge what it is; she has sworn me to secrecy."

He laughed and covered her hand with his own once more. "I shall look forward to seeing it. If Lady Silverwood has a hand in the matter the result can be none other than interesting."

"It is far from that, Matthew, but I must be guided by her taste which is far superior to mine."

He smiled at her indulgently. "My dear, Lady Silverwood has been out in Society for many years. By the time you have her experience you will also have superb taste."

She smiled gratefully. "Lady Silverwood has had many lovers, has she not, Matthew?"

"No more than other ladies of her station, but only one at a time which is considered a trifle eccentric." He paused before asking, "Do you happen to know whom she favours just now, Marin?"

In some distress she answered, "I cannot be certain, but it may be Sir Hugo."

Captain Ambrose drew a deep sigh. "So, I have a formidable rival."

She gave him a sad little smile and was glad when Lord Devaney came to join them, rendering that conversation impossible to continue.

It was some time later that Marin was being instructed in the game of whist by her brother and two other guests. As eager as ever to learn new skills she concentrated hard on the instruction but a new awareness in her caused an easy distraction, for wherever Sir Hugo went her attention wandered too.

She saw him walk over to where Lord Devaney was sitting on a sofa, finishing what remained of the excellent supper Sir Hugo had provided, and she watched them in conversation for a short while until her attention was reclaimed by her companions.

"I wish I could steal your cook," Lord Devaney remarked as his friend sat down beside him.

"You could not afford him."

"I expect to be in funds before very long."

He smiled engagingly at Sir Hugo who frowned in response. "It is time we called off this wager."

Lord Devaney was understandably taken aback. "You jest, Hugo."

The other man remained stony-faced. "It is not a matter for funning. I keep wondering what she would do if she discovered the reason we brought her to London."

"She will not, and we would have brought her in any event."

"She might not be able to comprehend that. Do you not think it time to call a halt to such foolishness?"

"Indeed I do not, especially as I am winning."

"Not quite fairly though. I have just learned that Captain Ambrose has provided his sister with a portion."

Lord Devaney was understandably taken aback. "A very modest one and not likely to weigh the odds any further.

Lieutenant Ripley is about to come up to scratch and would have done so in any event I am sure. He declares himself in love, and Miss Ambrose is kindly disposed towards him too."

Sir Hugo sat back in his seat, staring darkly at the object of the controversy and Lord Devaney added slyly, "You cannot always win."

"I shall rely upon Miss Ambrose's good sense so I may yet be the winner if it prevails. I just feel the introduction of a dowry for the chit may weigh the odds in your favour a little too much for my liking."

He eyed his friend coolly but Lord Devaney merely laughed. "How can you baulk at her modest portion? It was you after all who found Captain Ambrose. A rare error of judgement on your part."

At that moment Lady Silverwood came up to them, standing behind the sofa. Her brother looked up at her indolently. "My dear, Hugo wishes to withdraw from our wager, would you believe?"

"Oh no you don't, not when victory is in the wind. You would not be so dishonourable as to withdraw."

Sir Hugo rose to his feet. "It is a dishonourable business, Lady Silverwood, and I felt it was so from the beginning."

He strode away from them and she slipped into the seat he had vacated. Her brother chuckled before asking, "Do *you* experience any unease, Elspeth?"

She drew her eyes away from Sir Hugo and smiled at her brother. "I have grown fond of the chit and will be glad to see her settled for her own sake. She fancies she is a socialite now but it is far from so. She is still such an innocent. I will be happy when she has an adoring man to take care of her; it is what she needs above all else." Her eyes lingered on the group at the card table. "I feel we have done her a kindness whatever our original intent and perchance when it is over we shall reap our reward..."

"A thousand guineas, no less. All those who are dunning me will be paid in full."

She smiled faintly. "Not only that, Charles. This business has brought Matthew Ambrose into my life again."

Lord Devaney looked bewildered. "Captain Ambrose?" His sister's eyes grew moist and realisation came to him at last. "Dash it all, Elspeth, what about Hugo?"

Lady Silverwood waved her fan in the air. "Hugo, I am convinced, will remain a bachelor until the day he dies, whereas I do not wish to remain a widow for ever. I have quite suddenly discovered that there are other men in this world and I cannot be sorry for it!"

Her brother continued to look at her with surprise as she closed her fan and began to tap it thoughtfully against her lips.

"But Hugo's behaviour of late has me puzzled, Charles. Wanting to withdraw from this wager is quite out of character."

Lord Devaney looked smug. "He does not wish to lose."

"Hugo so rarely loses, I grant you, but when he does he accepts it cheerfully. In all the years we have been acquainted I have never known him to be a bad loser and a thousand guineas to Hugo is a very paltry sum."

"We may have been acquainted with him for many, many years, you and I, Elspeth, but I fear we shall never know him."

Sir Hugo was standing directly behind Marin's chair, a fact she was very much aware of. The game was difficult enough to master without her attention being distracted in this way. Even with her back towards him she felt his presence keenly. It was as if there was a magnetism in the air. She drew a deep shuddering sigh and feeling wicked she sat back in the chair to be closer to him. He did not move back and his hands were only inches away.

At last, unable to bear his silence any longer, she said in a high, nervous voice, "I do not seem to be able to master this game."

He moved then and she looked up at him nervously as he came to play her cards for her. Marin's hands trembled as he selected the correct card, after which he said, "We all have to learn, Miss Ambrose."

She laughed shakily. "You must all bear the eventual consequences of teaching me to gamble."

The other lady seated at the table laughed too, glancing at Sir Hugo. "When you are proficient you must play against Sir Hugo. That will be a true test of your prowess, my dear."

"I would not dare," Marin answered truthfully.

"Never be afraid of a challenge," he responded and when she looked to him again, he added in a voice no more than a whisper, "Who knows? You may just possibly win."

Ten

Shopping had become a more interesting pastime after Matthew allowed Marin pin money, and Lady Silverwood was very fond of visiting the shops for which London was famed. With the visit to Sir Hugo's house still clear in Marin's mind she, Lady Silverwood and Caroline wet off for a call on Lady Silverwood's favourite emporium which was situated in The Strand.

Each of them had declared the intention of purchasing some small items. Marin had decided to buy some cambric to hem and embroider for handkerchiefs, something she did prettily. The arrangements for the masquerade were well in hand and although Marin had looked forward to it because it was a novelty, now she eagerly awaited the evening simply for the fact Sir Hugo was bound to engage her for one of the dances.

As they set off she gazed out of the

window of Lady Silverwood's town carriage at Hyde Park which she thought looked so green and lovely in the June sunshine, although in truth everything about her seemed suddenly beautiful. Previously everything had been looked upon as a novelty, but now it was with a new awareness of life itself.

Soon she realised suddenly this Season would be over and she wondered then what she would do. Marin knew she need not really fear for her future; Lady Silverwood would surely never abandon her and even if she did there was always Matthew to rely upon. It was not this aspect which troubled her; sooner or later she would receive offers of marriage and it would be considered reasonable of her to accept one. The notion caused her untold pain, for she was not equipped to hide her feelings. Unlike other young ladies she would find it intolerable to marry one man whilst in love with another.

In love. The knowledge was both joyous and painful. For so long, when she read all those forbidden novels, she had wondered what it was to love passionately. Now, she acknowledged, there was a case for not looking for such an emotion in marriage, for she could not settle for less. Her sister, perhaps, was wiser than Marin had thought. Marriage for prosaic reasons was far more sensible. But there was no going back now.

The carriage was abreast with Tyburn and Caroline said to her mother, "Mama, when shall I be allowed to witness an execution?"

"Oh, you ghoulish child," Lady Silverwood complained and Marin's attention was drawn towards them. "Perchance, the next time you misbehave so it will be an awful warning to you."

"You must come too, Marin. It is something which you have not experienced as yet."

"Oh yes, I have," she retorted, much to the girl's amazement. "My father considered attending executions good for our moral fibre, but I assure you I would not have done so willingly."

"But it is so diverting at Tyburn! The condemned felons ride from Newgate on top of their own coffins, you know, and when they climb onto the scaffold they are allowed to speak to the crowd." The girl giggled. "Some of them are so afraid they dance about and the crowd boos them. If they are very brave they are cheered."

"Who has told you this?" Lady Silverwood demanded.

"Uncle Charles."

"I must have words with my brother. He is not a good influence on you."

"He goes back to the Surgeon's Hall to see them anatomised. He has promised to take me if only you would give your permission."

"Enough of this conversation, Caroline," her mother scolded and Marin hid her smile behind her hand. "You are incorrigible." She turned to Marin and confided, "Unfortunately I was far more precocious at her age so I have no cause to wonder whom she favours. But I often wish my husband was alive. I feel he might have had some cooling influence on her spirits although I dare say it would not be so. Men are always so intent upon their own pleasures and we women must attend to our children."

"I shall not," Caroline said pertly.

"I do not envy your husband, whoever he may be. He will be hard put to control you, my girl."

"You admit you were headstrong. I have often heard it said, but Papa loved you for it."

Lady Silverwood sighed. "Indeed that is

so. The years without him have made my pleasures less enjoyable."

Marin looked at her uncertainly. "You should marry again, Lady Silverwood."

She merely smiled sadly and then, glancing at Caroline again, Marin continued, "Bearing in mind my own childhood, Caroline's manner is not so terrible. At least she knows how to enjoy herself."

"But because you have come to pleasure late, do you not enjoy it all the more, my dear?"

Marin drew a heartfelt sigh. "There are moments when I wonder if it has all come too late."

Lady Silverwood was immediately concerned. "I cannot conceive that this is true. I believed you quite happy."

"I do not mean to seem ungrateful..." Marin hastened to assure her.

"I think she's in love," Caroline said. "She has the look of a moon-calf about her."

Marin was taken aback by the girl's acute observation, but her mother asked eagerly, "Is that so, my dear?"

She could not answer. Her passion for Sir Hugo was so foolish it could never be admitted but neither was it possible to deny.

When she turned to gaze out of the window Lady Silverwood let out a long sigh before saying in a carefully considered tone, "Your popularity is quite understandable. Such sweetness as is natural in you is very rare. I am convinced that within a se'ennight your future will be settled."

Marin managed to smile uncertainly in the hope of reassuring her mentor and it was Caroline who said, "Marin keeps her secrets close to her heart."

"That is quite understandable," her mother answered.

"When I am in love I shall be deliriously happy and want everyone in the world to know of it."

"Then it is fortunate we are not all like you," her mother retorted, and then she looked at Marin once more. "It is no secret that there are a number of men who desire you as a wife. Marin dear...perchance there is one of them you would accept with alacrity...You did one day indicate that Lieutenant Ripley..."

Marin had rarely felt so distressed. "I...have not given the matter much thought since then, Lady Silverwood."

"The time is fast approaching when you

will have to, and when you do you must also reflect that the chance will rarely come again. To have a man at one's side is a far more satisfactory state of affairs to being alone, and I speak as one who has known both situations intimately."

"But you have contrived handsomely."

The woman smiled wryly. "And I am only just now beginning to realise the folly of my ways. Besides, I am a widow which is different, and I was born into the Society in which I live."

"I do appreciate that I am but an outsider..."

Lady Silverwood was aghast. "By no means, my dear. Everyone acquainted with you has been enchanted, but because you are only recently arrived in London you have not been able to make many really close friends. Let me say that once you are wed I hope we shall remain friends and see each other often."

Marin smiled gratefully. "We shall, I promise."

Caroline was staring disinterestedly out of the window, but then she stiffened and peered out further, holding her hat on with one hand.

"Caroline, what are you about?" her mother demanded. "Put your head in immediately."

"I heard shouting and wondered what was amiss."

"That is nothing untoward. Someone or other is always shouting in the streets. It is most..."

As she spoke the carriage jolted to a halt, all but throwing the occupants off balance. "What is happening?" Lady Silverwood demanded of no one in particular whilst Marin attempted to peer out of the window at her side.

Caroline was wide-eyed. "I think it is a demonstration of some kind, Mama. How famous!"

"Nonsense. Demonstration indeed. Tucker! Tucker, what is the delay?"

"The road is barricaded by the military, my lady," the coachman called down. "We cannot proceed any further."

"We must; I have a deal of purchases to make."

"It would be best if we turn back, my lady."

"Oh, really," she said in exasperation and as she fumed the sound of shouting could clearly be heard nearby.

"They are chanting anti-papist slogans, Mama," Caroline told her.

"So, the Gordon faction is abroad once more. I cannot imagine what is happening to law and order. It is becoming increasingly common for the rabble to roam the streets, bringing inconvenience to law-abiding citizens."

"Surely something can be done about it," Marin said.

"If we are to believe what we are told, precisely nothing, but a very dear friend of mine is a member of parliament; I can see I shall have to have words with him."

"We cannot stay here," Marin pleaded, feeling thoroughly frightened now, for she was certain the shouting was growing louder and the soldiers who were attempting to man the barricades seemed to be doing very little to hold back the crowd.

Lady Silverwood looked affronted. "It would be foolhardy to allow this rabble to deter us from our course, Marin."

At the sight of a disreputable face at the window of the carriage Lady Silverwood let out a squeal of dismay. The creature, whether male or female was not very apparent, began to bang on the side of the carriage with an empty gin bottle.

"No Popery!" it cried drunkenly and Lady Silverwood shrank back against the squabs.

"Go away, you horrible creature," Marin cried and then, sitting forward, she hit out at him with her muff by which time the grooms had managed to chase him away.

"Let us go from here," Lady Silverwood cried, at last convinced of the sense of it.

"Can't move at all now, my lady," he shouted. "The devils have us hemmed in and there are too many abandoned carriages in the way."

She sank back into the squabs once more, closing her eyes. "We shall be overset."

Marin bit her lip in apprehension but just as the crowd began to surge about them there was a commotion on the box.

"They must have Tucker," Marin said fearfully.

"Oh, heaven preserve us!"

Caroline was still wide-eyed and flushed with excitement. "This is the most famous thing that has ever happened to me."

"Pray that it is not the last," her mother told her as the carriage unexpectedly jerked forward, turned sharply about and charged back the way they had come.

The three bewildered passengers held

tightly on to the straps as they were buffetted about inside, but at last the hands which clutched onto the bodywork of the carriage were obliged to release their hold.

"Tucker never drives like this," Lady Silverwood remarked breathlessly as she attempted to straighten her bonnet.

"I am glad he has discovered the ability," Marin answered, laughing shakily.

"I wish we could drive like this more often," Caroline said, chuckling.

"This carriage is not built for speed and not meant to be driven with such abandon. We are like to be overset at any moment."

"That danger, I am persuaded, is less than from the rioters," Marin pointed out.

Now that they were well clear of the commotion the carriage began to slow down and the passengers were able to sit up straight once more. The carriage had reached the Oxford Road which seemed a thousand miles away from the rioting, although it was only a mere mile and it came almost to a halt. The ladies were so intent upon tidying themselves that when the door flew open and a dark figure threw himself inside they were alarmed once more.

Within a few seconds the carriage had set

off again and the man seated himself next to Caroline. Lady Silverwood's eyes opened wide and she cried, "Hugo, So it was you who drove us away. I should have known the style!"

He allowed himself a small smile. "I thought you might." Encompassing them in one glance he asked, "I trust that none of you is injured?"

Immediately they assured him that this was so and whilst Marin could only gaze at him in awe, Lady Silverwood actually began to scold him.

"Really Hugo, are you aware we might have been overset by such recklessness?"

"I have never yet overset a carriage, and you had best concern yourself with what I did succeed in doing and that was to deliver you from that mob. I have, you may know, told your coachman my opinion of his dilatory behaviour. He was quite able to drive away; it was craven fear which stayed his hand."

"I think we were all afraid," Marin ventured and his glance rested on her momentarily which caused her to lapse into silence once more.

"Sir Hugo," Caroline said coquettishly, "I think your driving was quite splendid and I would wish to ride with you more often at such a pace."

He smiled at her. "That can easily be arranged, my dear."

The girl's face suddenly grew strained when she caught sight of Marin. The colour had drained out of her cheeks and the inside of the carriage began to swim before her eyes.

"Mama! Marin is going to swoon!" she cried.

Lady Silverwood called, "Stop the carriage, Tucker!" and reached into her reticule for a vinaigrette but it was Sir Hugo who acted most promptly. He reached forward to thrust her head down towards her knees, holding it there whilst Caroline made a feeble attempt to hide her giggles.

His prompt action had the desired effect; the dizziness abated and the world grew more still. When at last she was able to sit up again the colour was already returning to her cheeks but her most acute feeling was one of embarrassment.

"I am so . . . sorry," she murmured breathlessly, only aware that Sir Hugo still remained at the edge of his seat gazing at her only inches away. "That was exceedingly foolish of me."

"Nonsense, my dear," Lady Silverwood sympathised. "It was quite understandable. Even I must own it was an exceedingly frightening experience."

"You are not used to such terrors," Sir Hugo assured her.

"I cannot conceive why there should be such violence on the streets."

"Intolerance," he answered, smiling slightly. "You should know a good deal about that, Miss Ambrose."

At this observation she sighed. "Oh, indeed, but surely it cannot be allowed to go on."

"I am afraid that it might if no one is sufficiently resolved to end it. We must prepare for worse to come."

"Such lamentations," Caroline giggled, glancing coyly at Sir Hugo. "I find it hugely diverting, I confess."

"Only someone as foolish as you, Caroline, would consider it so," he admonished, but to Marin's astonishment the girl was not abashed.

"You will not consider me foolish in a year or two's time."

He smiled suddenly. "I would not wager upon that, Caroline."

"Ten guineas says you will adore me."

"Caroline!" her mother cried in horror, but Sir Hugo merely said, "It will be the easiest wager I have ever won. Let it stand. Shall we say three years from now?"

"You will be my slave by then," she said mischievously.

"No woman has yet contrived to perform that miracle." Lady Silverwood chuckled then. "You are tempting fate by saying so."

He returned his attention to Marin. "How do you feel now, Miss Ambrose?"

She managed to smile but inside she was agonising over making a cake of herself in front of him. "I am quite recovered, I thank you, Sir Hugo."

"Good." He sat back at last and Marin felt she could breathe again. "I suggest that if you wish to continue your shopping..."

"Continue!" Lady Silverwood complained, "We have not yet begun."

"You should remain in Bond Street or St James's Street and forgo the delights of The Strand for the moment."

Lady Silverwood glanced uncertainly at Marin. "I think we had best return to Park Lane."

"Not on my account," Marin assured her.

"It was only a passing weakness and I am over it now."

"You were quite brave," Caroline pointed out, "calling to that creature to go away."

Marin smiled modestly and Lady Silverwood said, "Very well, Bond Street it shall have to be. Instruct Tucker, Hugo."

He did so and Lady Silverwood looked at him curiously. "I am still totally bemused. How did you come to be on hand?"

As the carriage set off once more he sat back in the squabs and folded his arms, and although her eyes were downcast Marin was aware that his were upon her.

"I had heard of trouble this morning and when I spotted your carriage making directly for the area in question I thought it prudent to pursue."

"I am glad that you did," Lady Silverwood conceded. "I only hope we have not inconvenienced your own plans."

He took out his pocket watch and glanced at it before putting it away again. "I was on my way to an appointment with my tailor. However, I pay the fellow sufficient to allow for an occasional late appointment."

"I shall instruct Tucker to drive you there immediately."

"It will not be necessary. My own groom has followed us since I took the ribbons."

When the carriage jerked to a standstill he said, "Ah, here we are. No doubt you ladies will find something to your satisfaction at Madame Lesinsky's."

He got out of the carriage the moment the lackey had put down the steps and proceeded to give his hand first to Lady Silverwood and then to Caroline, who gave him an impish grin as she stepped to the street.

"Do not forget your costume for the masquerade, Sir Hugo," she reminded him.

"The matter is in hand I assure you."

Marin hesitated to leave the carriage at first but when he looked at her she forced herself to get out. Her hand trembled slightly as she placed it in his. It seemed that he held it for much longer than was necessary but she suspected that this was merely a flight of fancy on her part.

"Miss Ambrose," he said softly so that only she could hear, "if I am late arriving at the masquerade I beg you reserve a dance for me."

She looked at him directly at last. His lips

were curved into a half smile, his eyes beseeching. Her heart soared but when she noted Caroline watching them with interest Marin murmured, "I shall be honoured, Sir Hugo," and he released her hand.

Lady Silverwood paused in the doorway of the draper's emporium. "Hugo, I shall always be in your debt."

"Nonsense. If one cannot help an old friend..."

"Old indeed!" she retorted with mock indignation. "Come girls, let us depart."

Marin smiled at him shyly and followed Lady Silverwood but she could not prevent herself pausing in the doorway to glance back at him. He raised his hat but there was no telling expression on his face.

As Marin went into the emporium he caught hold of Caroline's arm and drew her back towards him. "You were wanting to drive in my carriage, Caroline..."

"Oh yes, indeed, Sir Hugo, but I didn't truly believe that you meant it."

"I am an honourable man who would never go back on his word. Let us discuss whether it will be in the curricle or the phaeton."

Caroline clasped her hands together in ecstasy. "Sir Hugo!"

Marin smiled to herself and as she turned to follow Lady Silverwood into the shop she wished for once she could change places with the child.

Eleven

Marin looked doubtfully at her reflection in the mirror, turning this way and that. Perched on the bed Caroline gazed at her too.

"It does look rather plain," Marin murmured.

"Mayhap, Mama wishes to ensure you will not look more beautiful than she."

Marin laughed. "No one could be more beautiful than your mother, Caroline, in any costume."

"Oh, I do wish *I* could go to a masquerade. It would be so romantic."

Marin smiled at her kindly. "The time will come when you will be able to enjoy every diversion."

"I cannot wait, but by that time you will be a respectably married lady. Shall you marry Lieutenant Ripley?"

Marin looked at her in alarm. "I . . . wish everyone would stop asking me that question. Whether I marry or not is only of importance to me. Besides, he hasn't offered for me and may not do so."

Caroline smiled knowingly. "Everyone expects that he will. Mama cannot wait for it to happen. I think she hopes to marry Captain Ambrose once you are settled."

Marin came to the bed and stood over Caroline. "What makes you think she would like to marry my brother?"

"Oh, I listen a good deal to what is being said and I know my Mama."

"What about Sir Hugo?"

The girl shrugged. "He is not anxious to marry and she has fallen in love with Captain Ambrose. I don't think she and Sir Hugo are very well suited and I believe Mama is becoming aware of it at last. He is a treacherous lover and although Mama appears to be a flirt and like only pleasure, she is also constant in her affections. Sir Hugo had a mistress who lived in Highgate, but when he tired of her she married a soldier and followed the drum."

Marin turned away. "Caroline, I do not wish to know such things, and if your Mama heard you speaking so she would be very angry. Such thoughts are not befitting a girl of your age."

Caroline gurgled into laughter. "Your costume is befitting your nature, Marin." When she walked away the girl asked, "Do *you* not find Sir Hugo attractive?"

Carefully Marin answered, "He is pleasant enough. You seem obsessed by him, but there *are* other men, Caroline."

"Lieutenant Ripley for instance?" the girl asked slyly and Marin drew a sigh of profound relief.

"Yes, indeed."

"You must own it was exciting having Sir Hugo rescue us as he did the other day."

"Caroline," Marin answered in desperation, "I have a great deal for which to be grateful to Sir Hugo."

Aware that her heated tone caused the girl to look at her speculatively Marin turned away again and began to toy with one of her brushes, silver-backed and a present from Matthew. The incident Caroline had spoken of had taken on a dream quality and it was not her own fear which remained uppermost in her mind; it was Sir Hugo's part in their rescue. She could readily understand Caroline looking upon him as a hero; Marin continued to do so also, nor had she forgotten that he had already bespoken a dance with her and the fact that he had done so made the evening an even more exciting prospect.

Caroline suddenly chuckled. "'Tis to be hoped all Mama's guests are able to arrive safely. There are demonstrators on the streets again tonight."

Marin looked up in alarm. "They are not in this part of town, are they?"

"Not yet, but that is not to say they will not be."

Marin became uneasy at the thought. "Can no one stop the rioting?"

"I heard Uncle Charles saying that no magistrate can be found who will read the Riot Act and so the military cannot act. I confess it sounds strange to me."

Marin's face relaxed into a smile. "To me too."

There came a knock on the bedroom door. A maidservant who entered on Marin's summons regarded her appearance with apparent disfavour before saying, "Lady Silverwood requests your presence downstairs, ma'am."

Caroline scampered from the bed as Marin scooped up her mask, taking a deep breath. "Good luck," the girl whispered. "I shall be waiting to hear all about it when you come up."

"It will be far too late," Marin told her as she hurried towards the door. "You should be in bed by that time."

"I could not possibly sleep. I want to miss nothing!"

"You never do whether you are present or not. Your methods, I confess, astound me."

Caroline gave her one last cheeky grin, adding, "You'd be surprised at some of the things I know, even concerning *you*."

This last remark caused Marin to pause, but Caroline was by then running away along the corridor and shrugging her shoulders, she hurried down the stairs to join the others.

Despite the turbulence in the streets of London Lady Silverwood's mansion was thronged with people, all dressed in fabulous costumes culled from history or mythology, and some merely from the imagination.

Although she was in constant demand Marin was never too occupied to be aware that Sir Hugo had not yet arrived. He had not been expected at the small dinner party which had preceded the masquerade but nevertheless Marin worried that perchance he had been waylaid by the malcontents who at present roamed the streets, and because of it could not fully enjoy herself. Her eyes continuously scanned the crowds for a sight of him.

There was something else to nag at her too. Earlier, when she had come down to join Lady Silverwood and Lord Devaney, the latter dressed in a glittering harlequin costume, he did at first regard her own costume with a frown, but then he came forward to greet her warmly.

"Marin, my dear, how charming you look." As Marin felt he was being less than sincere she could only smile faintly at his praise, but then he went on, "Good news. This afternoon at my club Lieutenant Ripley approached me..." Her heart began to thump uneasily. "I do not think I need elaborate upon the subject of our conversation."

"He has come up to scratch," she said in a whisper, almost to herself.

"The matter has been in his mind for some time but now you have a portion to your name he needs to hesitate no longer."

She turned away in distress to meet the satisfied look on Lady Silverwood's face. She had chosen to wear an Elizabethan costume and with her red hair piled high she cut a very regal figure.

"What did you say in reply?" she asked, addressing Lord Devaney once again.

"Naturally, I informed him that he must ask permission of your brother and he is resolved to do so at the earliest possible moment."

Marin had turned away so as to hide her dismay which they could not possibly understand. She was not certain she could understand it herself. Lieutenant Ripley was a fine young man and she had great regard for him. He would be a kind and considerate husband. Only weeks earlier she felt certain she would have accepted his offer with alacrity, but now...

Now, whenever she was not engaged to dance with another, Lieutenant Ripley was always in attendance, assuming her already to be his. As they sat together on a sofa near the dance floor Marin was fully aware of Lady Silverwood's smile of approval as she regarded her from the doorway.

"Miss Ambrose," the young man ventured, "perchance Lord Devaney has mentioned to you that we talked today..."

Nervously twisting her hands together she nodded her head.

"Needless to say, I intend to restrain my ardour until I have talked with Captain

Ambrose and obtained his approval, but my dear Miss Ambrose, I beg you to give me some indication that you regard me favourably."

Marin swallowed nervously. "How can I fail to do so, Lieutenant Ripley? I am exceedingly flattered by your attentions."

The young man seemed more than satisfied by her ambiguous answer and out of the corner of her eyes she caught sight of a figure which looked suspiciously like her brother approaching them.

At that moment it seemed imperative to keep the two men apart—at least until her thoughts were more coherent—and she said quickly, "Lieutenant Ripley, do you think you could procure for me a glass of lemonade?"

He was on his feet in an instant and as he went to the ante-room where refreshments were available Captain Ambrose came to join her, looking decidedly rakish in the costume of a pirate.

"We have had scant chance to talk this evening," he said as he sat down beside her.

"You, I have noted, have been dancing attendance on Lady Silverwood," she answered with mock reproach.

"I cannot keep away from her. I have

been wondering if it is too soon to declare myself."

"Does she indicate regard for you?"

Captain Ambrose laughed. "She is like a butterfly. Just when one thinks she is trapped she flits away."

Marin looked at him mischievously, wondering whether to trust Caroline's information. Certainly the girl seemed to know the truth of everything—or nearly everything.

"You can lose nothing by trying. You are not a callow youth, frightened of being refused."

"I do believe you are right, my dear. The worst thing I could do is dither. By the by, I note Lieutenant Ripley has been close at hand all evening. Lord Devaney has warned me to expect a visit from him although he suspects the young man might try to persuade me to increase your portion!"

Marin looked to him in alarm. "I hope you will refuse!"

Captain Ambrose smiled. "My dear, if you wish to marry him I shall be only too pleased to comply." When Marin did not answer he went on to ask, "You would like me to accept his offer, wouldn't you, Marin?"

"*You* would like to do so, wouldn't you?"

"It would be an excellent match, and I am not alone in thinking so. We cannot expect anyone of high aristocratic rank, but he is very well-connected. Lady Silverwood and Lord Devaney are quite unanimous in their praise of the man." He paused before adding, "But the final word must come from you, my dear. No amount of our approval will do if you do not look upon him favourably, but having observed you together I have no reason to doubt you have high regard for him."

"But if he wishes you to increase my portion, Matthew."

"That is no barrier, I assure you."

"I will give my answer when he has formally approached you and not before," she answered with a sigh.

Captain Ambrose seemed satisfied enough and she had not the heart to tell him the truth of her feelings. "Since my injury in the War I do not take to the dance floor very often, but I think I would like to stand up with you for this gavotte, Marin."

"I should like nothing better, but Lieutenant Ripley will be returning any moment with my lemonade."

"He is so moonstruck he will be content enough to wait until we have finished."

She demurred no further and allowed him to lead her to the dance floor where other couples were assembling. As they awaited the start of the music Matthew eyed her critically.

"When I first set eyes upon you in that costume I was quite taken aback by its severity, but since I have noted the attention you are receiving I have no quarrel with Lady Silverwood's choice."

The music struck up and the dancers began to move. Marin was aware of Lieutenant Ripley hovering near their seat, a glass of lemonade in his hand. Inconsequentially she thought she could not imagine Sir Hugo dancing attendance upon any woman in that way. Life, she discovered, philosophically, was totally unfair, for if she had encountered Lieutenant Ripley first it was likely her dilemma would not have arisen.

After the dance had ended Matthew returned her to Lieutenant Ripley's company and went immediately to join his cronies in the card room, and as he walked away Marin was glad to note that his leg did not seem to trouble him overmuch. She was just about to make some inconsequential remark to her companion when she caught sight of Sir Hugo at last. Masked or not, she could never mistake him for another.

He was standing near the doorway with Lady Silverwood and the sight of him caused her heart to leap. Marin did not care what anyone thought of her; she could not take her eyes from him. He looked so splendid. Almost everyone present had excelled themselves, but Sir Hugo's choice of a Cavalier costume suited his rakish looks perfectly. What is more, the costume was almost an exact copy of the one worn by his ancestor in the portrait at Lytton House.

Lady Silverwood looked at Sir Hugo deprecatingly. "I believe you had decided to snub us tonight."

"You know me too well to believe such a thing but it is fortunate that I arrived at all. All is up out there now, you know."

All at once she became concerned. "Is the trouble growing worse?"

"It could not be worse than it is now," he answered grimly. "Newgate, I am told, is ablaze and all the felons have been freed to join the rioters. In addition gin stores have been broken open and they are roaring drunk. It is no longer a cause they are shouting; 'tis only violence for its own sake."

"Is no one taking steps to end it yet?"

"At present it would seem not. Without the support of the government the military is helpless."

Lady Silverwood took a sharp intake of breath. "George Gordon should be confined to Bedlam where at least his antics would be amusing."

Sir Hugo took his first opportunity to look around the crowded ballroom and after a moment for the first time his lips curved into a smile.

"I am delighted to see the trouble in the streets has not hampered anyone's enjoyment."

"It would take a revolution to do *that*!"

Suddenly he caught sight of Marin who was still gazing in his direction. He caught his breath and following the direction of his gaze Lady Silverwood looked amused and said, "Are you also going to scold me about Miss Ambrose's costume, Hugo?"

"By no means, Lady Silverwood," he breathed. "It is a stroke of genius."

"Ah, I thought you might agree."

Amidst a glittering shifting tapestry of bejewelled costumes, towering headdresses and imagination run riot, Marin stood alone in a simple black gown with a white collar and cuffs as a Puritan. The effect was quite startling.

Sir Hugo started towards her but Lady Silverwood detained him a moment longer. "By the by, Hugo, you may be interested to learn that Lieutenant Ripley has come up to scratch at last."

He stared at her for a long moment before asking in a terse voice, "Has she accepted?"

"Not yet, but you needn't doubt that she will. Do you intend to pay up when the betrothal is announced or after the wedding?"

"We shall have to discuss that later," he snapped before striding away, leaving her to laugh gaily at their victory.

He went straight up to Marin, bowing low over her hand. "I trust you have reserved this dance for me, Miss Ambrose."

It was an effort to keep her lips from twitching with amusement but she did contrive to say in a straightforward manner, "It would depend very much upon who you are, sir. Behind your mask it is difficult to tell."

"I recognised you immediately."

Smiling wryly, she answered, "I do not doubt it. Lady Silverwood's daughter regards the costume as characteristic of my nature."

"Well, I do not."

Still amused, Marin put her head to one side. "And who may you be, sir?"

"It is Sir Hugo Lytton, Miss Ambrose," Lieutenant Ripley told her in a shocked whisper.

Marin laughed. "If that is so, I believe we *are* engaged to stand up for this dance."

The young man was left still holding the glass of lemonade as Sir Hugo led her on to the dance floor. Suddenly all her uncertainty was gone. Every opportunity to be in his company must be enjoyed to the full, and this she was resolved to do.

"There is a coincidence in our costumes, is there not, Sir Hugo? Yours a Cavalier and mine from the opposing side."

His eyes twinkled merrily behind the mask. "Do you really believe in coincidence, Miss Ambrose?"

"It can be nothing more, for our costumes were a great secret and I cannot believe Lady Silverwood would tell."

"Not Lady Silverwood, but her daughter

can always be persuaded, given the proper inducement."

Marin recalled his conversation with Caroline outside the draper's emporium and she stiffened slightly. "I only wonder that you should trouble, Sir Hugo."

The music started up and he answered, "Mayhap before long I shall tell you."

She was caught up in the music and dancing but she had the sudden feeling he admired her at last as a women. The memory of that would have to last throughout her marriage to Lieutenant Ripley, for it was likely now she would have to accept rather than invite the questions her refusal of his offer might invoke. He was a decent young man and she knew they could live in tolerable happiness together, but she couldn't help reflecting that her marriage would not be so very different from the one she had run away to escape. Loveless on her part and arranged by others. It was true that Lieutenant Ripley was not remotely like the man chosen by her brother-in-law, but she could never now enjoy the kind of ecstasy she had dreamed about for so long.

Twelve

The night was a balmy one lit by a full moon, a silver orb which hung low in a cloudless sky. In the garden of Silverwood House the troubles besetting parts of the city seemed far away, but Marin was only too aware that it was very close. But she had not escaped into the garden to ruminate on that. For a while she merely wished to be alone, to come to terms with the course of her life. Her adventure had come to its conclusion and she could reflect that she had enjoyed it except for the fact that the wrong man was involved, but philosphically she realised that nothing was ever perfect.

Soon it would be time to unmask and the sky would be filled with an explosion of fireworks which she was to view here with Lieutenant Ripley. She wondered if he would kiss her tonight in the shadow of the shrubbery and if he did, what her response would be. In the novels she had read the heroines invariably found it pleasurable.

All around her shadows moved. There was whispering and laughter and she knew many others were enjoying love's reward away from the eyes of the world. Marin wandered further into the garden, enjoying the sweet-scented night air after the oppressive atmosphere which prevailed inside the ballroom. As she strolled aimlessly two lovers laughingly ran across the path in front of her, causing her to draw back and then, realising she had come further than she had intended, she began to walk towards the house once more.

Suddenly a lone figure loomed before her in the shadows and she stopped on the path, her heart beating fast.

"Sir Hugo," she said in a low voice.

"So you recognised me on this occasion," he mocked.

"Your costume is the only one of its kind at the masquerade."

"Yours too, and it becomes you very much indeed."

Marin was glad that the dim light hid her blushes. "How odd that you should be out here too."

"I must be honest with you; I saw you slip out and took the opportunity of following."

Almost involuntarily she stepped back a

pace. "I needed some air."

He was smiling slightly. "'Tis as well. It would have been embarrassing for me had you come on an assignation with a lover."

She hesitated to pass him on so narrow a path but her heart beat the faster when he came a few steps closer. He reached towards her and she drew back even further.

"Allow me to remove your mask."

"It is not time," she answered hurriedly. "We must wait for midnight."

"It is past midnight."

"That cannot be so."

"I assure you that it is." Regardless of her protest he began to untie the ribbons and feeling foolish she could only stand there and allow him to do it.

"That is better," he said, stepping back and scrutinizing her face carefully. "I had a fancy to see your face."

"Everyone will be coming out at any minute now for the firework display."

"Ah, you do not know. It has been cancelled. In view of the rioting Lady Silverwood has decided it would not be prudent to put on such a display."

At this revelation Marin did make to go past him. "If that is so I must return to the ballroom."

Sir Hugo put his hand on her arm to

detain her and she looked up at him fearfully. "Grant me a few moments of your time. There is something I would wish to discuss with you."

She continued to gaze up at him and she was certain he was able to hear her heart thumping noisily within her breast. "I cannot conceive what that might be."

His eyes seemed to possess almost an hypnotic quality, for she could not look away. "Is it true Lieutenant Ripley has made an offer for you?"

She was forced to avert her eyes then. "He is about to approach my brother, I believe."

"Would it be presumptuous of me to ask what his answer will be?"

In a voice no more than a whisper Marin answered, "Matthew will allow me to decide for myself, Sir Hugo." She raised her eyes to his once more. "Why are you so concerned to know?"

"Can you not guess?" he asked and his voice was very soft in her ear.

Marin's thoughts wheeled round in her head. Her senses told her the moment was a dangerous one and that she should go, but her legs were incapable of carrying her. Before she could collect her thoughts sufficiently to go, with one practised move he swept her into his arms. He looked down into her face for a long moment before he bent his head to kiss her. She closed her eyes and melted into his arms, making no pretence of a struggle.

When he drew away from her she said in wonder, "I have never been kissed before."

"Your lips were meant to be kissed, little puritan, but I am glad to be the man who has the honour first."

He kissed her again, this time his lips caressing her face and neck and she clung on to him, rejoicing in the feel and the warmth of his body so close to hers.

"It is fortunate Lieutenant Ripley has forced me to declare myself," he murmured against her cheek.

"I am glad too," she sighed.

"Do you love me?"

"Yes, yes I do. Madly. Wickedly."

Holding her very close to him he answered, "There is nothing of madness or wickedness about what we feel. It is glorious."

"I was convinced that you were in love with Lady Silverwood."

"She and I have enjoyed a long-standing rapport but that is all."

"I am so glad; not just for my own sake but for Matthew's too. He is in love with her."

"And they are well-matched, almost as well-matched as you and I. Oh, I am going to enjoy indulging your every whim. You shall have everything in the world you desire."

"How can you speak of such matters at this moment? If I have you it is all I could ever wish for."

He held her away a little. "I know it and your total lack of acquisitiveness is one of the reasons I love you, but even so I shall enjoy lavishing everything upon you. You must not try to stop me."

She laughed. "As your wife, it will be expected of me, but it is you I really want. Nothing else."

He drew away from her again and sensing a withdrawal in him her eyes narrowed speculatively. "Have I said something wrong?"

His answer was an uncomfortable laugh. "There is nothing wrong, save that you go too fast for me. Tonight we have both made a wonderful discovery but we must get to know each other a little better before we discuss marriage."

"I... am... beginning to understand," she stammered. "I was, I think, being too presumptuous."

He laughed again as she freed herself from his embrace completely. "You have not been presumptuous; it is merely that I have led a bachelor existence for so long 'tis impossible for me to adjust to anything else for now, but we shall see each other far more often than most married couples do." He attempted to draw her close to him again. "How could I stay away from you for long?"

As he came to take her in his arms once more she backed away from him. "And what of the time you grow weary of my company? Or if you find another more to your fancy? What then, Sir Hugo?"

"It will never happen. I shall never tire of you."

"You tired of the doxy you kept at Highgate," she countered and was rewarded by his look of surprise and before he could answer all her anger and heartbreak came spilling forth. "How dare you class me in such a way? Have you forgotten I have a brother to look out for me?"

"Marin, you are quite wrong..."

"If I tell Matthew what you have proposed tonight he will call you out."

His eyes grew suddenly dark. "If you have a care for him you will not and in any event he would have better sense than to do so. No man has ever got the better of me in a duel."

"Oh, you are always so sure of yourself it is not to be borne, but be certain you will not have your way in this instance."

"Have you quite finished?" he asked in a steely voice.

Her answer was to lift her skirts and make to pass him. Her entire body was trembling with emotion and for the moment she could not trust herself to utter another word.

"*Honi soit qui mal y pense,*" he murmured as she fled through the garden. She was relieved that he did not pursue her but she was choking back her tears, aware that only pride kept her from him.

Many of the guests were beginning to depart, much earlier than usual owing to the desperate situation outside which worsened with every hour, something Marin was not fully aware of at that moment. Even if she were, she would only have heeded the turbulence within her own heart.

As she hurried through the hall where Lady Silverwood was bidding goodnight to her guests Marin did not stop and the other woman gave her a curious glance. Marin hurried up the stairs and was relieved at last to reach the sanctity of her room, relief which was only fleeting for Caroline was there waiting for her.

The moment Marin came inside the room the girl sprang to her feet and Marin said wearily, "Caroline, I am much too tired to have a coze tonight. In fact I have a headache and want only to go to bed."

The girl smiled. "Well, that is not so surprising. It has, after all, been an eventful evening."

Marin gave a broken little laugh, before asking, "Caroline, do you know what *Honi soit qui mal y pense* means?"

The girl shrugged. "Of course. It means, 'evil be to he who evil thinks.' It is the motto of the Garter Knights. Why do you ask?"

Marin turned away to hide her troubled expression. "I...just heard someone say it."

Caroline came up to her. "Do you intend to accept Lieutenant Ripley's offer?"

Marin had sunk down onto the bed but now raised her eyes to meet Caroline's. "He is yet to make it," she sighed, "but everyone is agreed that he is an excellent young man and I am not likely to receive a better offer."

Caroline's eyes sparkled maliciously. "So Sir Hugo has not managed to change your mind after all?"

Marin was completely taken aback. "What...what do you mean?"

The girl's eyes strayed towards the window. "I was waiting for the firework display and saw something of far greater interest."

"It was nothing," Marin said wearily.

"I am sure that it was, but I must confess I was not surprised that Sir Hugo attempted to dissuade you from marrying Lieutenant Ripley. It was entirely predictable that he would, but the method he used was rather contemptible."

Marin's eyes narrowed with interest. "Why?"

"Because of the wager. If you marry Lieutenant Ripley Uncle Charles wins and Sir Hugo will lose."

"What are you talking about, Caroline? What wager?"

The girl looked smug. "The wager on you. Had you no notion?"

"No! What do you mean? Explain yourself, Caroline."

"I told you I knew a great deal about you. The wager is the reason you were brought here in the first place. Uncle Charles, you see, said you would find a husband by the end of the Season but Sir Hugo wagered a thousand guineas that you would not. Now you can see why Sir Hugo made that attempt to sway you tonight. He had nothing to lose, but I am persuaded if you had been swayed by him, you would soon have been discarded."

"I cannot credit this!" Marin cried, wide-eyed.

"'Tis true nevertheless."

Her thoughts were milling around in her head whilst Caroline studied her with interest. "It is strange that he did not contrive to persuade you to change your mind about Lieutenant Ripley, for Sir Hugo has an easy way with women."

Marin shook her head in distress and her voice was choked with emotion. "Oh, do go away, Caroline, and let me rest."

The girl went slowly towards the door. "I know I should not have told you about the wager, and they will be furious with me for doing so, but it was unfair of them to use you as they did. At least," she added cheerfully, "it has not affected the outcome of your romance with Lieutenant Ripley."

As soon as she had gone Marin sank

down onto the counterpane, silent sobs racking her body. To think she had actually believed them considerate of her to bring her to London! Lord Devaney and Lady Silverwood had seemed so sincere. And Sir Hugo. She could scarce bring herself to think of him now. He was the most depraved of men. There had to be a fund of wickedness inside her own soul to be attracted to him.

In her frustration she hammered silently on the counterpane whilst a flood of tears soaked into it. Some time later as she lay on the bed motionless and numb there came a knock on the door. She did not answer but nevertheless moments later Lady Silverwood let herself into the room.

When she saw Marin, still dressed and lying across her bed, she hurried to her. "My dear, what is the matter?"

She sat up then, glaring at the woman accusingly. Her eyes were very bright but dry now. "Please leave me alone."

"Are you ill? Only tell me and a physician will be summoned, although I would not dare to guess which one of them will venture out into the streets tonight. I am now preparing rooms for those who wish to remain until morning." She sat down on the counterpane next to Marin. "Now, dear, tell me what ails you."

It was all Marin could do not to flinch away from her. "I thought you were my friend, Lady Silverwood."

"And so I am and always hope to be. What makes you think I am not?"

"The wager. You have taken me up only because of the wager."

For a moment there was silence and Marin did not dare to look at her. "The wager..." Lady Silverwood echoed at last.

"Caroline told me of it tonight."

The older woman twisted her fan between her fingers. "I declare I shall strangle that child." Then she turned to Marin. "Oh, my dear, I am so sorry you found out. We meant no harm but men do gamble on the oddest eventualities and when my brother solicited my help I could not refuse."

"I do understand, Lady Silverwood."

"Oh, you do not! And I cannot blame you for it. 'Tis a shameful thing but all is ended happily."

Marin looked at her at last and her eyes were bleak with misery. "Has it?"

"Why yes. As a direct result you have

found your brother and a husband too. Matters have turned out famously, you must own. I have grown exceedingly fond of you," she added gently, "and believe me, my dear, I would not for the world have seen you hurt by this silly wager which means so very little to both men."

Lady Silverwood rose to her feet and stood by the bed, looking down at her. "Try not to think too badly of us and do have some rest. By the morning I am certain you will see that you have not lost by what has happened."

Marin did not answer but when the woman had gone she jumped to her feet and began to gather together a few personal belongings, tying them in a neckerchief before fetching a cloak from the press. Taking a deep breath she hesitated inside the doorway before slipping out and along the corridor to the servants' staircase.

When Lady Silverwood returned to the drawing room where some of her guests remained she beckoned immediately to her brother who was at that moment enjoying a game of picquet. The hard-pressed servants were serving an extra supper to those who could still manage to eat more. Sir Hugo was surprisingly sitting alone, gazing into space and apparently oblivious to the activity and conversation all around him. Lady Silverwood, however, was too perturbed to consider it odd.

She waited impatiently for her brother to join her and when he did so he said, "Poor Elspeth, this evening has not turned out as you would have wished."

"Not in any way," she snapped. "Charles, Marin has learned about the wager. Caroline has told her."

Lord Devaney looked understandably shocked. "Caroline! How the devil did she know?"

"She eavesdrops but that is not the point."

Lord Devaney continued to look dismayed. "I do not suppose the girl is pleased."

"She feels *betrayed* and I cannot find it in me to blame her. She is so vulnerable, Charles; she is not hardened to such matters as we are." She glanced to where Sir Hugo was slumped deep in thought. "I dread that Hugo finds out. It is what he feared and he will be furious."

"To the devil with Hugo! What if Captain Ambrose finds out? It will be pistols at dawn."

"Fortunately he has already left to secure his house against the rioters but she is bound to tell him."

Lady Silverwood bit her lip and no more could be said, for two of their acquaintances intruded, but she continued to look troubled. Some time later her brother drew her to one side once more.

"Elspeth, I have been thinking on this matter. You had better let me have words with Miss Ambrose. Perchance she will accept apologies from me and we may avert trouble. I have no fancy for a duel with Ambrose."

"When I spoke to her she was in no mood to be approached and now she has retired for the night, so it will have to wait until the morrow."

Lord Devaney's hand tightened on her sleeve. "No, dash it all, it will not do on the morrow. I want to speak to her before she has a chance to see Ambrose. I do not have to tell you it will not only be a duel between us but the end of your hopes to become his wife."

A spasm of pain crossed her lovely

features before she took a deep breath. "Very well. I shall entreat her to join you in the library but I cannot guarantee that she will."

He waited impatiently in the hall for his sister's return which came only a few minutes later. "Charles!" she cried as she hurried down the stairs. "She is not in her room. She has gone!"

It was at this moment that Sir Hugo came out of the drawing room. The lackey outside closed the doors behind him and as he did so Sir Hugo became aware of the tension between his two friends.

He looked at them questioningly. "What is amiss?"

"Marin," Lady Silverwood answered in a strangled voice. "She is gone."

Sir Hugo stiffened. "Gone where?"

"I don't know. She is not in her room and no one has seen her leave, so it may be that she used the servants' staircase."

"Why should she choose to go out at this hour of the morning?"

"Ah," Lord Devaney said in a muted tone, "I think you should know Miss Ambrose has learned of our little wager. Caroline told her."

"Hell's teeth!" he swore. "I'll make that

brat smart for this."

"You needn't doubt she will be punished," Lady Silverwood answered in a muted tone, "but what is more pressing is the need to find Marin."

"My God, if she's out there...!"

Lord Devaney shrugged. "Where can she have gone?"

"To Matthew's... Captain Ambrose... where else?" Lady Silverwood answered.

Sir Hugo's eyes flashed with pain and emotion. "The mob is still running amok all over London." He started forward. "I must go and find her. If any harm befalls her..."

Lord Devaney caught his arm. "Steady on, Hugo. You cannot go. It is too dangerous and it is not your place."

Sir Hugo levelled a furious stare at his friend. "It is very much my place and if you wish to be helpful prime me a brace of pistols, then have your curricle brought round. I shall try to cover the ground between here and Bloomsbury Square."

Lord Devaney did not move. He continued to look doubtful. "Do it *now*, Dev!" Sir Hugo urged and his tone sent the young man scuttling to instruct his servants.

The streets were awash with running,

shouting figures, many of whom were brandishing gin bottles looted from stores broken into earlier in the day. Now the majority were either drunk enough to riot or lying insensible in the gutters.

Marin ran this way and that to avoid the rabble which sped through the streets whichever way she turned. By now she had no idea where she was, even if she had wanted to return to Lady Silverwood's house.

It seemed like hours since she had left that safe haven and close to exhaustion she stumbled on drunkenly herself. Another group of drunken rioters were coming up the street and she shrank back into the shadows, hoping she would be overlooked, but a toothless old man caught sight of her and pulled her along with them. They were all mad, she thought, as they began to throw lighted torches through the window of one house, and Marin cried out aloud in protest but her voice was lost in the midst of the roar of delight which went up as flames began to shoot out of one window.

She tried to run away only to be enveloped by maddened drunkards once more. She twisted this way and that, trying to free herself but whichever way she turned she could not escape. It was a great temptation to lie down and rest but she suspected if she did so she was likely to be trampled underfoot or caught in one of the many fires erupting all over the city.

In the hope she would be left behind she clung on to some railings, but just when she thought she might have succeeded in her ploy a straggler caught sight of her. He slowed down, grinning hatefully as he swayed uncertainly on his feet and Marin attempted to pull her cloak more tightly about her. He caught hold of her by the shoulder and, leering lewdly, tried to rip it off. More terrified than ever, she screamed, but the sound of it was lost once more.

"Let her go!" demanded an authoritative voice.

The rioter turned and then, smiling again, he raised his cudgel. Marin also looked around, her eyes widening in amazement at the sight of Sir Hugo striding across the debris-covered street. She blinked for fear she was dreaming but it was indeed he, a greatcoat covering his rather conspicuous Cavalier costume.

As he approached the rioter dashed forward, his cudgel foremost. Marin's hand flew to her mouth and just when it seemed the man would strike Sir Hugo down there was a flash of fire and a deafening crack. The creature sank to the ground, blood seeping into the cobbles from a wound in his breast. At the sight of it she cried out again, staring at the rioter who was now either dead or unconscious.

Sir Hugo tucked the pistol into his waistband and it was then that Marin fell into his arms. Her grievance against him was now forgotten in her need for the comfort of his arms. Her reason for running away seemed so foolish now anyway.

More rioters were coming their way and he pulled her into the darkness of a doorway where they could not be seen. He shielded her trembling body with his until the danger was past and she was calm again.

"Are you hurt?" he asked in a harsh whisper.

"No. Heavens be praised, you came in time." He held her close again, his face buried in her hair until she asked in a slightly muffled voice, "How *did* you find me?"

"Pure good fortune. I have been scouring the streets for hours which has not been easy, for at the same time I have had to dodge the rioters. I was beginning to fear I would *never* find you."

"*I* have been running around for an age

too. It was terrifying. The world has gone mad."

"Most of them are not aware of any cause; they are just foxed out of their minds." He took her face between his hands and an expression of pain crossed his features as he looked down at her. "Why, oh why were you so foolish as to go out tonight?"

Her eyes filled with tears. "I didn't realise the situation was so bad and I just wanted to get away from Silverwood House as quickly as possible. I thought I would go to Matthew's house but the chair was overturned and the chairmen fled ..."

Her voice faded away at the memory of her terror and he began to kiss her. The danger, her anger towards him and his friends were forgotten with the delight his kisses created in her.

"I must get you back to safety," he said, drawing away at last. "We had best return to Silverwood House. Do you feel able to walk a little way?"

"Yes, but I have no wish to return to Silverwood House. I know ... about the wager and never want to go there again."

He drew in a sharp breath. "I am so sorry that you have been caused so much anguish. I knew no good would come of it but I am as much to blame as Dev."

She brushed back a few renegade curls from her grimy face. "I understand," she answered in a weary voice. "Gentlemen gamble on all manner of things and it was foolish of me to think you took me up out of kindness."

"Originally that was our only reason for doing so."

"Well, you might be relieved to know I do not intend to marry Lieutenant Ripley after all. He deserves more devotion than I am able to bestow upon him. You will win your wager after all, which is only just; I am not ungrateful for the services you have done me."

Sir Hugo looked about to reply but then he glanced out of the doorway and a moment later, with his arm tightly about her, they hurried along the street. The smell of acrid fumes hung in the air and there was a glow in the sky where buildings still burned. Every so often they were obliged to draw into the shadows to allow rioters past but at length reached the courtyard where Sir Hugo had concealed Lord Devaney's curricle.

He lifted her up into it and moments later the curricle was racing back towards the comparative safety of Park Lane. When they approached Silverwood House, Marin said mutinously, "I shall leave as soon as it is safe to do so. Somehow I don't believe I shall be welcome when I reveal my decision about Lieutenant Ripley."

The curricle jerked to a halt and throwing down the ribbons he swept her into his arms. "You will leave here with me—to become my wife and for no other reason."

She attempted to draw away from him in alarm. "Your wife? But only tonight..."

"I was uncharacteristically incoherent tonight, Marin, and when you mistook my intention I was angry enough to allow you to continue with your misapprehension. I regret it bitterly now. For weeks I have been obliged to fight my feelings for you but tonight when I saw you I could contain myself no longer."

"So it was not just to win the wager..." she said, looking at him in wonder.

"That never entered my head, I swear. It was you I wanted and still do but what I said to you was ill-considered and I knew it immediately. But it is of no consequence now. I do want to marry you and I cannot live without you a day longer."

"I am deeply honoured," she answered thoughtfully, "but, Hugo, there are others more fitted to be your wife."

222

"For fifteen years I have scorned every one you would consider suitable. I have waited a long time for you and I will not take no for an answer now, for I know you love me too."

Her lips were trembling but she could not prevent a smile. "You would lose the wager."

"Lose? I have won your love. What greater fortune can be mine?"

"It will cost you a thousand guineas."

He lifted her to the ground. "You are worth all the gold in Christendom so I have secured a veritable bargain." He slipped his arm around her. "Come, let us go inside so I can pay Dev his winnings. This must be the very first wager where everyone concerned is a winner!"